Books by Ellen Conford

The Luck
of
Pokey Bloom

The Luck of Pokey Bloom

by
ELLEN CONFORD

Illustrated by
BERNICE LOEWENSTEIN

Little, Brown and Company
BOSTON   TORONTO   LONDON

Library of Congress Cataloging in Publication Data

Conford, Ellen.
    The luck of Pokey Bloom.

    SUMMARY: A young girl learns that
winning and getting along with people
are often more than a matter of luck.

    I. Loewenstein, Bernice, ill.   II. Title.
PZ7.C7593Lu   [Fic]   74-26556
ISBN 0-316-153052

10 9 8 7

HAL
*Published simultaneously in Canada
by Little, Brown & Company (Canada) Limited*

PRINTED IN THE UNITED STATES OF AMERICA

The Luck
of
Pokey Bloom

1

**WIN THE HOUSE OF YOUR DREAMS!
ENTER THE POW ALL-PURPOSE CLEANER
SWEEPSTAKES
AND IN A FEW SHORT MONTHS
YOU MAY BE LIVING IN SPLENDOR
YOU NEVER DREAMED POSSIBLE!**

Pokey bit her lower lip in concentration, trying to fit her name, address, city, state and zip code into the little spaces on the entry blank.

Did she have a dream house, she wondered. She'd never thought about it before. She stopped writing for a moment and rested her chin on her pencil eraser.

Her house was okay, even if it was a little old, and maybe a little bit weird, compared to her friends' houses. Most of them had nice, up-to-date split-levels, or simple, one-story ranch houses; even the people who lived on Pokey's block, where most of the houses were

3

kind of old, had fixed them up so that they looked sort of modern.

But the Blooms' house was the only one on the whole block that still had a big front porch with a wooden floor and wicker furniture on it. And they still had striped canvas awnings on the windows that faced the afternoon sun. And Pokey's older brother, Gordon, had a room up on the third floor that was part attic, part tower, and the oddest shape.

Maybe her dream house was new. Brand-new, with nothing ever breaking and everything modern. Something was always needing to be repaired at the Blooms', and whoever came to fix whatever it was would always shake his head wonderingly and say, "Gee, I haven't seen one of *these* in years." Pokey was the only person she knew whose bathtub had little feet that raised it up off the floor. Her father kept saying it was old-fashioned and ugly, and they ought to modernize, but Pokey's mother, who was an artist, insisted that it had a certain charm.

One thing she would definitely have in her dream house — a room of her own big enough to hold a Ping-Pong table, a color television and a soda fountain bar with stools, where she could whip up thick shakes for herself and her guests whenever she felt like it.

But other than that, Pokey simply didn't have any ideas about what "living in splendor" might be. Well, she shrugged, if she did win, she could always talk it over with her parents. They were bound to have some suggestions.

Pokey made her letters as tiny as possible. The spaces they gave you were so small. She hoped the judges would be able to read her name and address when it came time to send her the prize. It would be terrible if they picked her entry and then couldn't tell whom to give the dream house to!

"Can you read this, Gordie?" Pokey shoved the entry blank at her brother, who was standing, arms folded, next to the hall phone. He glanced at it.

"Sure," he said absently.

"Gordie, you didn't even look!"

"Yes I did!" he snapped. "Listen, can't you see I'm busy?"

Pokey gazed at him leaning against the staircase wall, watching the telephone and doing absolutely nothing. *Busy?* Why, he wasn't doing a thing.

What in the world was the matter with Gordon these days? The helpful, caring big brother, whom Pokey had looked up to and liked, had been replaced by a grouchy stranger, who snarled instead of smiled and had no time to waste on her.

"It's just a phase he's going through," her mother kept telling her. "He'll get over it. Try not to let him upset you."

But he *did* upset her.

She stomped upstairs to her mother's room, feeling hurt and angry, the way she always seemed to feel lately whenever she tried to speak to Gordon.

Pokey's mother drew pictures for books, and was working on a pen and ink sketch for a book about insects.

"What do you think of this, Charlotte?" her mother asked as Pokey walked in. No one but her mother and her teachers called Pokey "Charlotte," which was her real name.

Mrs. Bloom held up the picture.

"Oh, that's really beautiful," Pokey breathed. It was so neat and clear and clean, the lines black and dramatic against the white paper. When Pokey drew pictures they were smudgy and scrawly, and she always tried to change them to get something right. Then they ended up looking worse than they had in the first place.

"What is it?" she asked.

"It's a cockroach," her mother said briskly. "And I agree with you. It's a pretty terrific cockroach."

"Can you read my writing?" Pokey asked, holding out the entry blank so her mother could see it. "Do you think it's too small?"

"Oh, Charlotte, not another contest? What are you going to win this time?"

6

"The house of my dreams," Pokey replied. "We may be living in splendor you never thought possible in a few short months."

"Sounds delightful," her mother said, peering down at the entry blank. "Yes, I can read it. It's small, but very clear."

"Oh, good," Pokey said. "I was worried."

"And what would your dream house be like?" her mother asked. She wriggled her fingers around to relax them.

"I'm not sure," Pokey said thoughtfully. "But I'd have my own soda fountain and a big room, and there would be no bathtubs with feet. Those are the only things I can think of that I really want."

Pokey's father appeared in the doorway. "You may get your wish," he said. He was red-faced, and his hands were grimy. He held a wrench and a dirty rag.

"As a matter of fact, that whole bathroom is going to be replaced one of these days, even if I have to rip out everything myself."

Pokey's mother held up her sketch.

"How do you like my cockroach?" she asked cheerfully.

Mr. Bloom always got angry when he tried to fix something around the house. The family was used to it. Sometimes he got very angry, and yelled and cursed and stomped around and ended up calling someone else to fix it, and sometimes he fixed it himself, but he *always* got angry.

"I love your cockroach. I'm crazy about your cockroach. But let me tell you about your bathtub. Your bathtub is one of the last relics of an ancient civilization whose plumbing secrets remain unknown to this very day. Perhaps the mysteries of their unique methods of constructing bathtubs, faucets and drains — not to mention toilets — will be unraveled when the archaeologists dig up the remains of this civilization. But UNTIL THEN," he bellowed, "that bathtub drain is going to LEAK!"

Pokey giggled. She really loved the way her father talked when he was angry; some of her friends' fathers just screamed and cursed, but her father, who was a high school teacher, yelled with real style.

Of course, she only found it funny when he was angry at *things*, like the bathtub or the furnace or the storm windows; it wasn't funny at all when he was angry at *her*, or her mother.

"Do you think we should call the plumber?" Pokey's mother asked calmly. She hardly ever got excited about things breaking.

"On Saturday? On Saturday all the plumbers are busy counting their money. You can't get a plumber on Saturday. Do you have any idea how much money they have to count up by Monday?"

8

"Even if they just counted the money *we've* paid them," Pokey's mother smiled, "it would keep them pretty busy."

"Very true," said Pokey's father. "A good point. Listen, I'm getting something to eat. Anybody want anything?"

"Not me," said Mrs. Bloom, picking up her pen again.

"I do," said Pokey, who was always ready to eat.

"Well, I just naturally assumed *you* would," her father said. "Let's go see what there is."

The phone rang — half a ring.

"My, that was a short one," Pokey's mother commented.

"Gordie was standing right by it," Pokey said. "He must have grabbed it."

Pokey and her father went downstairs. There was no sign of Gordon. And the phone was nowhere to be seen either.

"Look at that!" Pokey said, pointing to the trail of telephone wire that snaked under the phone table and across the hall floor. "He's in the closet! He took the phone into the closet with him!"

Muffled sounds came from behind the closet door.

"I guess he wants privacy," her father said, sounding amused.

9

The closet door flew open, and Gordie, hand over the mouthpiece of the phone, glared at them.

"Do you mind? I'd like a little privacy. Do you have to stand right there and eavesdrop?"

The door closed in their faces.

"Eavesdrop!" Pokey shrieked indignantly. "Of all the —"

"Shh, come on," her father said, steering her into the kitchen. "Pay no attention to him. He's a little sensitive."

"If you ask me," Pokey said sourly, "he's a little nuts."

"Well, maybe a little of that too," her father agreed, "but it will pass. In the meantime, we will tiptoe around the fringes of his life, and intrude as little as possible."

Pokey thought that was a lovely way to say it — even if she didn't know exactly what it meant.

"Now," her father said, peering into the refrigerator, "what's there to eat?"

After a snack of leftover tuna fish salad, potato chips and chocolate milk, Pokey got an envelope and a stamp from the telephone table and addressed her contest entry. The phone, she noticed, was back in place and Gordon was nowhere in sight.

Pokey walked to the mailbox, put her letter in, and checked to make sure it hadn't got stuck in the chute.

She crossed all her fingers, then crossed her arms one over the other. She also tried to cross her eyes, but that hurt, and she decided it wasn't absolutely necessary.

"I wish I would win," she muttered, screwing her eyes shut. "I wish I would win."

"Hey, Pokey, what ya doin'?"

Pokey opened her eyes and uncrossed everything that was crossed. George Fisher, who lived next door to the Blooms, was on his bike, trying to do wheelies.

"I'm giving myself good luck," she said. "I might win a dream house." She started back up the block. George pedaled slowly along beside her.

"What's a dream house?" George asked curiously. "Is it real?"

"Sure it's real," Pokey said. George, after all, was only eight. "It's a real house you dream of."

"Then it isn't real," George said.

"Yes it is," Pokey insisted. "After you get it, it's real."

"That doesn't make sense," George declared. He yanked the handlebars of his bike up as if he were riding a bucking bronco.

Pokey stopped trying to explain it to him. He was a nice boy, but just too young to understand some things.

"If I win my dream house," she said, "you can come and have a soda anytime you want."

George frowned at her, completely mystified.

Pokey went into her house and stopped short right inside the front door. The strangest noise was coming from somewhere upstairs. Her parents were in the basement; she could hear their voices drifting up through the open cellar door, so it couldn't be them.

Thump, thump, thud. Thump, thump, thud. What in the world could it be?

She went upstairs and looked in the bedrooms. Nothing. But the noise was louder up here. Definitely. Thump, thump, THUD. Thump, thump, THUD.

Pokey started up the half flight of steps to Gordon's attic room. THUMP. It was coming from there, she was sure of that now.

Slowly she tiptoed up the steps. What was going on in there? Was it a burglar? Was he beating up Gordon? Why wasn't Gordon yelling?

She leaned her ear against the closed door.

THUD. The floor shook.

Maybe it was Gordon, doing something.

"Unnff," came his muffled groan.

Pokey decided it was time to act. Gordon was certainly either in trouble or in pain. But she'd better be quiet and careful. If it were a burglar, maybe she could take him by surprise.

Thump, thump. "Umfff."

Pokey turned the doorknob, slowly, silently. She

pushed the door open an inch and peered inside the room.

There was no one in the room but Gordon. And he was balanced on his head on the floor, his legs and feet propped against a wall.

"Gordie! What are you doing?"

Thud! He fell over and his legs hit the floor.

"Oh, rats, Pokey. I just had it, too. What do you want?"

"I'm sorry. I heard this strange noise, and I thought —"

Her brother was setting himself back in place, head balanced in his hands, back and legs bracing against the wall. Thump, thump. That was his feet hitting the wall. He hadn't taken his sneakers off, and there were black smudges all over the white paint.

"Gordon, why are you doing that? Your face is getting all red."

"That's the blood rushing to my head," he gasped. "It improves circulation."

"Well, I don't know what that means," Pokey said doubtfully, "but do you think it's good for you to get all red like that?"

"What do you think I just said, dummy? Ooff." He fell forward again. Thud.

"Pokey, will you get out of here? I can't concentrate with you staring at me like that."

"I'm not staring at you," Pokey said. "I'm just watching you."

"Well, quit watching me!" His voice cracked. "You're making me nervous."

"Can I try it?" Pokey asked. "Would you show me how to do it?"

"If I show you once, will you get out of here?" Gordon demanded.

Pokey nodded.

She put her head in her hands like Gordon showed her, then let him lift her feet and legs and prop them against the wall. Her head hurt. So did her knuckles, because her hands were taking all the weight of her head and body and were pressed hard into the floor. Gordon let go of her legs and she felt herself being pulled forward, away from the wall. She fell over and her feet made the thudding sound Gordon's had.

"I almost had it, didn't I, Gordie?" she said, getting up. "Let me try it again."

"I said once," her brother growled. "Now, get out of here."

"Oh, come on, Gor —"

"I mean it, Pokey! Stop being such a pest; just leave me alone!"

Pokey glared at Gordon. She rubbed her head.

"If I win my dream house," she began furiously, "your room is going to be the dungeon."

"Your dream house!" Gordon sneered. "That'll be the day, when you win one of those stupid contests. Meanwhile this is *my* room, so get OUT."

Pokey whirled out the door and stomped down the stairs. She was close to tears, but she didn't want to give Gordon the satisfaction of seeing her cry. That was probably just what he wanted. Why else would he be so mean to her? He never used to act like this. Mean, and nasty and — *dumb*.

Making phone calls in closets! Standing on his head!

She turned and shouted up the stairs.

"You're dumb, Gordon! You're a big dope!"

Thud. She smiled nastily.

"And clumsy!" she added. She pictured him sprawled on the floor.

There. That took care of *him.*

2

Pokey had finished her arithmetic problems and was sitting in the class library corner thumbing through a magazine. Mr. Nader let you pick out something to read if you finished your work before the others did, so Pokey and her friend, Bethanne pulled their chairs close together so they could look at each other's magazines at the same time. That wasn't like the two of them reading the same book, which Mr. Nader didn't like at all, since he said they ended up talking and giggling instead of reading.

WIN THIS VALUABLE TRANSISTOR RADIO!
COMPLETE WITH PERSONAL EARPLUG!
TAKE IT WITH YOU ANYWHERE!
WORKS ON ONE NINE-VOLT BATTERY!
(Not included.)

Just what Pokey wanted! Her own personal transistor radio that she could take with her anyplace. She could even have music while riding on her bike, just like a car radio. A bike radio.

Pokey read on.

You can win this transistor radio for your very own just by selling boxes of Happy Days Greeting Cards to your friends and neighbors! Happy Days Greeting Cards are so easy to sell, they practically sell themselves! Your customers will be pleased with the beauty and variety of Happy Days Greeting Cards; they will surely want several boxes to keep on hand for those special occasions. In no time you will have sold enough Happy Days Greeting Cards to win your transistor radio. Just fill in the coupon below and we'll send you all you need to start you on your Happy Days way.

Pokey hurried to her desk to get a pencil and paper. She didn't think she ought to tear the magazine coupon out, so she copied the address of the Happy Days Greeting Card Company onto a piece of paper and stuck it in her skirt pocket.

"Look at this," Bethanne whispered, as Pokey went back to her seat near the books. She held out the magazine she was reading, the *Junior Observer*, and pointed to a picture story.

The story was about a group of Girl Scouts who had

18

gone on an anti-litter bike hike; they had cleaned up the lakefront area in their town, and riding there on their bikes and back they had scoured the route of the cycle path for trash, cleaning it up as they went.

"What are you looking at?" whispered Nora Priddy, squeezing a chair between Pokey and Bethanne. They pushed their chairs a little apart to make room for her.

Mr. Nader looked up and frowned at them. Bethanne put a finger to her lips, as if to assure him that they would be quiet, and held out the magazine so Nora could see it.

"Why don't we do that?" Bethanne whispered.

"We don't have a dirty lake," Pokey said.

"We could clean up the park," Bethanne suggested.

Mr. Nader came over to the library corner.

"You know this isn't a talking area. It's a reading area."

Bethanne pulled the magazine away from Nora and bent her head over it. Pokey tried to look interested in a story about starfish in her own magazine.

Nora grabbed a book from the shelf and opened it right to the middle.

Mr. Nader walked away.

"They don't let bicycles in the park," Nora muttered, barely moving her lips. Her head was still buried in the book.

"Anyway, the park is very clean."

Bethanne frowned. "I'll think of something," she breathed. "It's still a good idea."

After lunch Pokey, Bethanne and Nora sat under a tree in the schoolyard sharing the remains of Nora's little box of raisins.

"If only we could think of someplace messy," Bethanne said thoughtfully. "We could get all the girls in the class together and ride down there and clean it up."

"Why can't we just all get together and ride someplace without cleaning it up?" Pokey asked.

Bethanne shook her head. "It's not the same," she said firmly. "What a shame everything around here is so clean."

Pokey giggled. Bethanne sounded so unhappy that their neighborhood wasn't littered with beer cans and Popsicle wrappers and old boots.

"Hey, I have an idea," Nora said suddenly. "You know that big lot behind the school bus garage? That's always a mess. It's practically a dump. All kinds of garbage gets thrown there."

Bethanne's eyes lit up. "Oh, that's a great place to clean!" she exclaimed. "It's really filthy!"

"That's kind of far away," Pokey said doubtfully. "I've never ridden so far on a bike before."

"Come on," Bethanne said, ignoring Pokey's worry. She jumped up and brushed off her skirt. "Let's go get

all the girls and see who wants to come. We can go next Saturday."

When she came home from school Pokey found her mother in the kitchen.

"How was school today?"

"Fine. Listen, Mom, we're all going on a bike hike to clean up the lot behind the school bus garage and everybody's going, Nora and Bethanne, and all the girls in the class, we're all going together, can I go?" Pokey had to stop to catch her breath.

"Oh, Charlotte, I don't know. That's a long way to go on a bike from here."

"You mean, I can't go?" she asked anxiously.

"Well, now, honey, I didn't say you couldn't go, I just —"

"Then I *can* go?" Pokey cried, jumping up from her chair.

"No, I didn't say that either," her mother answered.

"Well, can I or can't I?" asked Pokey desperately.

"I'll think about it," her mother said. "And talk it over with your father."

"That means no," Pokey grumbled.

"It doesn't mean no, it means I'll think about it," Mrs. Bloom corrected. "Now why don't you go change your clothes and play outside for a while?"

Pokey's shoulders slumped in defeat. She was sure

that she heard "no" in her mother's tone, despite Mrs. Bloom's promise to "think about it."

She trudged up the stairs. She'd probably be the only girl in the class who couldn't go. They would have a wonderful time, and maybe even get their pictures in a magazine, like the Girl Scouts who cleaned up the lake, and she would be the only one who had to stay home because she wasn't allowed to ride so far from her house.

Pokey pulled off her skirt and sweater and dropped them on a chair in her room. A piece of paper was peeking out of her skirt pocket, and she pulled it out, curiously.

It was the address of the Happy Days Greeting Card Company that she had copied from the magazine. She pulled on a pair of slacks and a shirt. Then she sat down at her desk and tore a piece of paper from her homework notebook.

She would send for her greeting cards right away. She would sell enough to win the transistor radio. The thought of winning her own radio temporarily took her mind off the bike hike — until she heard the front door slam, and her father calling, "Anybody home?"

Pokey raced downstairs to meet him.

"Mom has something to talk to you about," she announced breathlessly, flinging herself at him and hugging him.

"What broke?" he asked suspiciously, hugging her back. "I have a hundred and twenty test papers to mark. It had better be something simple enough for a child to fix."

"It's nothing like that," Pokey reassured him. "Nothing is broken."

"Nothing is broken?" he repeated, as if he didn't believe it. "That doesn't seem possible. In this house something is always broken. Are you sure?"

"I'm sure," Pokey grinned.

Her mother came to the hall, where they were standing, and kissed Mr. Bloom.

"Talk to him now," Pokey urged. "Ask him."

"Ask me what?" he wondered. "Pokey, you look very anxious about something."

"She is," Mrs. Bloom said, "and I'm not at all sure it's a good idea."

"Well, if she wants to join the Marines, it's okay with me. As long as that's what she *really* wants."

"Oh, Daddy, it isn't that!" Pokey groaned. Her father was very funny, but sometimes he fooled around *too* much.

He followed Mrs. Bloom into the kitchen, Pokey trailing after him.

"What are we eating?" he asked eagerly.

"*Boeuf miroton,*" she said grandly.

"Leftovers, right?" he guessed.

"How did you know?"

"When you say it in French, it's always leftovers," he explained.

Pokey hopped impatiently from one foot to the other.

"*Please,*" she begged, "talk about it *now.*" What did it matter what they were having for dinner? Didn't they realize what was really important?

Pokey's mother repeated what Pokey had told her about the bike hike.

"The thing that bothers me," she concluded, "is that it's so far to ride, and across so many main streets. It's not the same as riding right around here, or to Bethanne's house."

"But we'll all be together," Pokey pointed out. "That's the main thing. It won't be dangerous if we're all together. And we can walk our bikes across the big streets. I'll walk my bike across *every* street, if you want, I promise."

Her father looked solemn. He was going to say no.

"Maybe I could drive you to the —"

"Oh, no!" Pokey wailed. "That's no fun! Everybody else will be riding over. I want to go with *them.*"

"They *will* be all together," her father said to her mother.

"I know," she replied. "That's the thing. It's not as if she were going alone."

Pokey looked unbelievingly from one to the other. They sounded as if they were on her side! They were talking as if they were going to let her go.

"It's for a very good cause," Pokey added hopefully. "And I wouldn't get run over by a car when there's a lot of us."

"That isn't funny, Charlotte," her mother said sternly.

"I wasn't being funny," Pokey said. "It's true."

"Safety in numbers," her father commented. "It's a good point."

Pokey couldn't believe it. They were going to let her go! She flung her arms around her father's waist and hugged him hard.

"I don't know," he sighed doubtfully. "On the whole, I think I'd worry less if you were joining the Marines."

Saturday morning at breakfast, Pokey hurriedly gobbled down her scrambled eggs, glancing at the clock every few minutes. She ate so fast that she was finished before everyone else, and it was still too early to leave.

Gordon was prodding at his eggs with a fork.

"Are you going to eat them," his father asked cheerfully, "or are you trying to stab them to death?"

Gordon pushed his plate away. "I can't," he said.

"Why not?" asked his mother. "Don't you feel well?"

"I feel okay. I'll have some toast, I guess. And cereal."

"But Gordon, I made three eggs for you. You always eat three eggs. Why don't you want them?"

"I don't know if vegetarians eat eggs," he replied.

"Vegetarians?" his father repeated.

"What's vegetarians?" Pokey asked.

"People who don't believe in eating meat," her mother explained. "Gordon, since when are you a vegetarian?"

"I just *am*," he said irritably.

"But that's not meat," Pokey pointed out. "That's eggs."

"Look, stop making a big thing out of it," Gordon said. "I'll just have some toast and cereal." He got up to get the bread and milk.

His parents looked puzzled, Pokey noticed, but she was too excited about the bike hike to wonder about Gordon now.

The phone rang. Gordon leaped up from the table and raced to answer it.

He came back into the kitchen. "It's for you," he said glumly to Pokey.

Who could it be, Pokey wondered, going into the hall. It's so early.

"Hello?"

"Hi, Poke," Bethanne said, sounding very annoyed. "Listen, we can't go today."

"Can't go?" Pokey cried. "Why not?"

"Joanne has a virus or something — anyway, she's throwing up a lot. Tina has to go to the orthodontist — she forgot about it. And Nora has a rehearsal for her dance recital."

"Well, why didn't they tell us before now?" Pokey said angrily. "I was all set."

"So was I," Bethanne said.

"What about tomorrow?" Pokey asked.

"Tomorrow I have to go to visit my aunt in Connecticut," Bethanne said. "I thought we could try again next Saturday."

"Okay," sighed Pokey. " 'Bye."

She went back into the kitchen and slumped into a chair, her shoulders sagging with the weight of her disappointment.

"Problems?" asked her mother.

"We're not going," Pokey replied.

"Oh, that's too bad, honey," Mrs. Bloom sympathized. "And you were looking forward to it so much."

"Yeah," Pokey agreed.

"Listen," her father said, "if you're really anxious to do something about cleaning up your environment today, I have about four hundred pounds of leaves that

I was going to rake this morning. You can help me with that."

"That's not the same," Pokey grumbled.

"No, it isn't," her father admitted cheerfully, "but it's a rotten job, and I need the help."

"Why can't Gordon help you?" She looked around. Gordon was gone.

"Good question," her father said. "And if I ever find him, I'm going to ask him that very thing. Well, we might as well get started."

He pulled himself out of his chair.

"Would you prefer raking or bagging?" he asked, grandly offering Pokey his arm.

"Oh, I don't care," she sighed, getting up and linking her arm with his. "Whichever you don't want to do."

"Perhaps a little of both," he said. "You know the old saying about variety being the spice of life."

Well, thought Pokey, there were worse ways of spending a Saturday than with her father.

Of course, she reminded herself gloomily, there were better ways, too.

3

GORDON was squatting on his heels, his hands on his knees, his eyes bulging. His mouth was stretched so wide his chin nearly touched his chest. His tongue was stuck out as if the doctor had told him to say "Ahhh."

Pokey gasped.

"Gordie, are you having an attack?"

Gordon's features relaxed into their natural position, which, these days, formed a scowl.

"Don't you know how to knock on a door?" he demanded.

Pokey tapped on the door she had just opened.

"Can I come in?"

"No," he said. "I'm busy."

"Gordon, what are you doing? Why are you making those faces?"

"I'm taking up yoga, if you're so curious," he said. "That was one of the positions."

"Why are you taking up yoga?" Pokey asked. "Why do you have to sit like that?"

"Because yoga is a healthful way to promote vitality of mind and body. Now, will you please get out of my room?"

"I just wanted to remind you that Mom's birthday is tomorrow," Pokey said. "I thought you might have forgotten."

"Boy, no one around here trusts me to have the brains of a two-year-old!" he snapped. "Dad's told me every day for the past week not to forget Mom's birthday, and now you —"

"All right, all right," Pokey said hastily, backing out of his room. "I just thought —"

"And close that door!" Gordon yelled.

Pokey slammed it as hard as she could.

She went down to her mother's room.

"Gordon is still being a pain," she announced bitterly.

But Mrs. Bloom was hunched over her worktable, frowning. Pokey didn't think she'd even heard her. Now was obviously not a good time to repeat her complaints about Gordon.

"I'm going out for a while, Mom," Pokey sighed.

"Okay, dear," her mother replied absently. "Don't be gone too long."

Pokey looked over her mother's shoulder at the illustration she was working on. It was a picture of a ladybug.

"That's nice," she said admiringly. "I like the little dots."

"Thank you, honey," Mrs. Bloom murmured, hardly moving her lips. "They're so small, I have to be careful."

"Well, see you," Pokey said. She was glad that her mother was concentrating so hard that she forgot to ask her where she was going.

Pokey ran down the stairs, feeling the three dollars she'd saved from her allowance comfortably wadded up in her pocket. In her other pocket was her entry in the Brewmaster's Black Forest Bock Beer Sweepstakes. The grand prize was a dune buggy, which she thought would be a wonderful thing to have.

She closed the front door softly behind her and hurried down the porch steps.

"Hey, Pokey, where ya going?" George yelled, screeching his bike to a stop in front of her.

"Shh!" Pokey put a finger to her lips and glanced nervously toward her mother's window.

"I don't want my mother to hear us."

"Why not?" George whispered loudly.

"I'm going to buy her a birthday present," Pokey said. "Her birthday is tomorrow."

"Oh," George whispered. "Can I go with you?"

"All right," Pokey agreed, "but we're not going to fool around. I have to be back in time for dinner, and I don't want to be gone so long that she starts asking questions."

"I won't fool around," George said, sounding insulted.

He dropped his bike carelessly on the front lawn and they started off. Pokey stopped at the mailbox on the corner to drop her contest letter in. She closed her eyes tightly, crossed her fingers, and wished.

"I wish I would win," she muttered. "I wish I would win."

"What are you going to win now?" asked George.

"A dune buggy," Pokey answered. "I *hope*."

"Wow," George sighed. "That would be neat."

"What are you going to get your mother?" he asked, as they crossed Providence Place.

"I don't know," Pokey said thoughtfully. "I couldn't get any good ideas, so I thought I'd just look around and see what they have. I ought to be able to get something nice for three dollars."

"You could get her perfume," George suggested. "I bet you could get a really big bottle for three dollars."

"I don't know," Pokey said as they walked into the five-and-ten. "Everybody gets perfume. It's not a very original idea."

"My mother likes perfume," George said.

They walked past a display of kitchen utensils.

"How about this?" George asked, holding up a vegetable grater. "This is very useful."

"No," said Pokey. "That's not for a birthday."

She looked on the other side of the counter, where there were pots, kitchen clocks, coffee makers, and mixing bowls.

"How about a coffee pot?" George suggested.

"We have a coffee pot," Pokey said impatiently.

Over in the next aisle there was a display of plastic flowers and plants.

"Hey, these are really neat," George said. "They're fake. Look how real they look. I'll bet your mother would like a bunch of flowers."

"Yeah, but not fake flowers," Pokey said. "She doesn't like that stuff."

"My mother likes it," George remarked. "She has a whole bowl of fake green leaves in the dining room. With fake lemons in it too."

Pokey and George walked up and down the aisles. Nothing she saw excited Pokey at all, and she wanted something special for her mother, a present that would mean something. It should be a gift just right for her, and shouldn't be the kind of thing you would give to just anybody.

They had been past every counter but one, and Pokey was beginning to lose hope. George thought everything was interesting, and kept making suggestions. Pokey had to practically drag him away from the toy counter, which was the one place where he didn't see anything that he thought her mother would like. He just saw a lot of stuff *he* liked.

The last aisle had jewelry, and Pokey walked slowly past the display, her eyes moving carefully from object to object, not wanting to miss a thing. This was her last chance to find something in this store, and she didn't think she'd have time to go wandering around the shopping center if she couldn't find a gift here.

She was almost at the end of the jewelry counter when she saw it. It was perfect. It was beautiful. And so *appropriate*, Pokey marveled.

"That's a bug!" George yelled as she picked it up.

"Isn't it wonderful?" Pokey murmured, gazing at it. It was a pin shaped like a ladybug, and very small — no bigger than a dime. It had little gold feet, and it was enameled in dark red with tiny brown dots.

"But, it's a *bug*," George insisted. "Why do you want to get your mother a bug?"

"Because it's perfect," Pokey said.

The salesgirl came over to them. "Can I help you with something?"

"Yes. I want to buy this." Pokey held out the pin, which was attached to a piece of white cardboard.

"That's a dollar ninety-eight," she said. "Plus fourteen cents tax."

36

"That leaves me enough for a card and wrapping paper," Pokey said happily. She handed the salesgirl her three dollar bills. The woman took the money and ran up the sale.

George couldn't stop shaking his head.

"I bet she'd rather have perfume," he said worriedly.

Now Pokey had to pick out a birthday card, and that took a long time too. Like the gift, the card had to be just right, and there were so many to choose from.

Finally Pokey found what she wanted for her mother. It said HAPPY BIRTHDAY MOM on the front, and it had a picture of a little puppy with a pink bow around its neck. Inside, the verse was:

> *You do so much for all of us,*
> *And everything you do,*
> *Makes us realize there's not*
> *Another Mom like you.*

That was exactly how Pokey felt, so she bought the card and a package of wrapping paper, and a little white gift box to put the pin in.

As they came out of the five-and-ten, George gave Pokey a shove with his arm.

"Hey, look, there's your brother," he said, pointing down the row of stores.

Pokey peered in the direction of George's finger and saw Gordon leaning against a store window.

"What's he doing?" asked George.

"I guess he finally decided to buy my mother a birthday present," Pokey replied disgustedly. "Boy, talk about waiting till the last minute."

"Well, why is he just standing there?" George demanded.

"I don't know," Pokey shrugged. "Let's go ask him."

Just then Gordon turned around, looked furtively over his shoulder, and hurried into the store.

"He must be buying Mom's present in there."

"In *there*?" George repeated. They walked down the row of shops to the one Gordon had entered. "What kind of a present can he get in there?"

They stood in front of the store window and gazed at the sign.

Hermes' Health Food Heaven
Natural Foods
for a Beautiful Body.

"I don't get it," George declared.

Pokey just stared at the display in the window and shook her head.

"Me neither," she replied. "Maybe he's going to buy her some health food."

"That's a dumb present," George said scornfully.

"Well, that's what Gordon is these days," Pokey said. "Dumb."

It wasn't till nine that night when Pokey remembered the bike hike was the next day. She groaned in disappointment, thinking of the cake she had planned to bake, and all the preparations for the birthday dinner she and her father would have to make.

She trudged to the phone and called Bethanne.

"Guess what?" Pokey began, when Bethanne answered.

"Don't tell me," her friend sighed. "You can't go, either."

"What do you mean, either?" asked Pokey.

"Nora has another rehearsal. And Tina has whatever it was Joanne had. I don't think this thing will ever get off the ground."

"Oh, that's a shame," Pokey said. But she was inwardly relieved that they weren't going to go without her.

"You'd think we could all get together, just one day," Bethanne grumbled.

"Maybe next week?" Pokey suggested.

"Who knows?" Bethanne replied gloomily. "Until Nora's recital, she'll probably be having rehearsals every Saturday. And somebody's bound to get sick."

"Well," Pokey said uncertainly, "it's still a good idea."

"Yeah," Bethanne said. "Well, I'll keep working on it."

The next morning, while her mother slept late, Pokey and her father went to the supermarket to buy food for the birthday dinner. Mr. Bloom was going to cook, and Pokey was going to bake the cake.

They got a roast beef, devil's food cake mix, instant fudge frosting, which came in a can, artichokes, celery and olives, and brown & serve rolls.

When they got home, Pokey's mother was in the kitchen having a cup of coffee.

"Happy birthday!" Pokey shouted, dropping the bag of groceries she was carrying onto the table, and running to hug her mother.

"Thank you, honey," Mrs. Bloom said sleepily. She gave Pokey a quick hug. "You two are up early."

Mr. Bloom put his bag of groceries down. "Happy birthday," he said cheerfully. "Hurry up and get out of the kitchen."

Mrs. Bloom blinked a few times and poured herself another cup of coffee.

"I just got up," she yawned. "Give me a minute to open my eyes the rest of the way."

"Oh, don't rush her, Daddy," Pokey protested. "It's

her birthday. She should sit in the kitchen and drink coffee as long as she wants." Pokey glanced nervously at her mother. "You won't be *too* long, will you?"

"I'm finished, I'm going," her mother said, gulping down the rest of her coffee and putting her cup in the dishwasher.

Pokey grinned at her father and they began to put the food away.

"I'm going to start making the cake right now," Pokey decided. "I want to be sure it's cool before I frost it. If you put the frosting on too soon it melts."

"Okay," he said. "I'll prepare the celery and the olives and get the artichokes ready for cooking. That way, all I'll have to do tonight is the roast and the potatoes."

Pokey began to read the directions on the back of the cake mix box. But right beneath the instructions, Pokey saw something else.

WIN $10,000 IN OUR REDIMIX CAKE MIX CONTEST! JUST COMPLETE THE FOLLOWING SENTENCE IN 25 WORDS OR LESS:
"I use REDIMIX CAKE MIXES because . . ."
Entry blank inside this package.

Ten thousand dollars! Pokey whistled softly.

"What is it?" her father asked.

"You can win ten thousand dollars," Pokey said excitedly, "just for telling why you like this cake mix in twenty-five words or less. Ten thousand dollars!"

"You could use the money, eh?" her father asked.

"Boy, could I!" Pokey agreed.

"Couldn't we all," he muttered, trying to make the electric can opener work.

Pokey sat down in a kitchen chair and stared at the cake mix package. Ten thousand dollars!

"Maybe you'll get some ideas for the contest if you make the cake first," her father hinted.

"Oh. Yeah."

Pokey gathered her mixing bowl, the electric beater and an egg. She read the directions again, trying to keep her eyes from straying down to the tantalizing contest announcement.

It was very easy to make the cake. All she had to do was add an egg and some water and beat the batter for three minutes with the electric mixer.

She greased two cake pans and poured the batter into them, trying to get an equal amount into each pan. It didn't come out quite even, she thought, but it was pretty close.

She preheated the oven, and rinsed out the bowl and the beaters and stuck them in the dishwasher. Her father was trimming artichokes and humming.

Why do I like Redimix Cake Mix? Pokey asked herself. Well, it's easy. It's fast. But all cake mixes were

42

easy and fast. Pokey didn't think those reasons were original enough to win ten thousand dollars.

She put the cake in the oven and set the timer. She stuck the entry blank in a kitchen drawer and went upstairs.

Her mother was making the bed in the master bedroom.

"Why are you working?" Pokey asked. "It's your birthday. You're supposed to relax and have a good time. I'll make the bed."

"Honey, you don't have to make our bed. Just do yours. I'll do this one."

"No," Pokey insisted. "I'll do yours *and* mine. It's your birthday."

She finished making her mother's bed, while Mrs. Bloom looked around as if trying to find something to do. Then Pokey went into her own room and made the bed. She did a much less careful job on her own than she had on her parents', but she wasn't that fussy about the way it looked.

In half an hour the cake was ready to come out of the oven. One layer was a little higher than the other, and it tilted a little, but Pokey didn't think it would matter — she could cover everything up with the icing.

Just before lunch a package came in the mail for Pokey. The return address said "Sunshine Paper Products." Pokey couldn't imagine what it was. She tore at the wrapping eagerly, until she succeeded in working off the paper and the tape, and found a cardboard box inside with a letter on top of it.

"Here is your sample box of Happy Days Greeting Cards," the letter read. "We're sure your friends and neighbors will be thrilled with their beauty and charm. Your prize list is included. Read it carefully. Take your orders on the enclosed order forms, and remit with check for amount of boxes ordered. Good luck!"

Pokey opened the box and looked at the cards. There were all different kinds, for birthdays, for sick people, for moving to a new house. Pokey wasn't sure that her friends and neighbors would be thrilled by the beauty of the cards; they looked pretty much like all the other cards she saw in the five-and-ten. But she was sure that it would be very convenient not to have to go to the store every time you needed a card, and maybe people would like that.

Anyway, she *had* to have that transistor radio, and she was sure she could sell enough boxes to earn it.

"Pokey, you'd better get that cake finished," her father said later on in the afternoon. "It's almost dinnertime. Is your present wrapped?"

"Yes. I did it last night."

"I'd better check on Gordon," her father said. "He's been in the closet with the phone for an hour. You'd think he'd have to come out for air once in a while."

"He's pretty touchy," Pokey warned. "He says we act as if he doesn't have the brains of a two-year-old."

Her father started to say something, but changed his mind.

"Well. If he's still in there talking by the time you finish the cake, I'll cut the telephone wire. That ought to get his attention."

Pokey opened the can of frosting and went to work on the cake. It was fun, and didn't take long at all. The cake still tilted a little, but it looked very nice.anyway.

Pokey wrote HAPPY BIRTHDAY, MOM with a tube of yellow decorating gel. It made a bright contrast with the chocolate frosting. She stuck a little yellow candle in the center of the cake.

"There," she said, stepping back to admire her work.

"Beautiful," her father said. "Really beautiful. Now, if we can just get your brother out of the closet, we can have dinner."

Pokey went to get her present from her desk drawer. She ran into Gordon on the way downstairs.

"Hurry up, Gordie," she urged. "We're all waiting for you."

"All right, all right," he grunted. He continued up the stairs at the same snail's pace. Pokey made a horrible face at his retreating back and raced down the rest of the stairs and into the den.

Her mother was watching the six o'clock news on television.

"Come on, Mom," Pokey said, grabbing her arm. "Everything's ready."

"Oh, good," Mrs. Bloom said, sounding very relieved. She switched off the television and followed Pokey into the dining room.

Gordon had just come downstairs, and was putting his present in front of his mother's plate at the head of the table. Pokey put her present on top of Gordon's and sat down.

"Isn't everything beautiful," Mrs. Bloom admired.

"I set the table," Pokey told her. Gordon scowled.

"Open your presents," Mr. Bloom said. He sounded almost as excited as if it were his own birthday, Pokey thought.

Pokey could hardly sit still as her mother unwrapped her present.

"Oh, look at that!" Mrs. Bloom cried. "Isn't that the cutest thing!" She took the ladybug pin out of the box and held it up against her sweater to see how it looked.

"Oh, Charlotte, how clever!"

Pokey beamed. "Remember the ladybug you were doing for the book?" she asked.

"Of course," said her mother. "That's why this is so perfect."

She pinned it onto her sweater and looked down at it, smiling.

She opened Gordon's gift next. Gordon watched his mother carefully as she pulled off the paper.

"Oh," she said brightly. "Isn't that interesting. Tropical Fruits Natural Fragrance Bath Crystals."

"All natural ingredients," Gordon pointed out. "You won't get allergies from *that*."

Mrs. Bloom, who didn't have allergies, nodded. "My, don't they smell delicious."

She passed the box to Pokey, who took a sniff.

"Smells like Hawaiian Punch," Pokey said. Gordon glowered at her.

"I'm going to use them tonight," Mrs. Bloom declared.

"If you can get the bathtub to work right," Pokey added.

"Thank you, Gordon. It was very thoughtful of you."

The next two packages were from Mr. Bloom. "Open that one first," he said, pointing to the larger one.

Eagerly, Pokey's mother tore off the wrapping paper.

"Oh." Mrs. Bloom looked at the gift inside. It was a pink metal box equipped with a set of screwdrivers, pliers, and assorted tools.

"You always said," Pokey's father pointed out, "that you could fix things if only you had the right tools."

"Yes," Mrs. Bloom said shortly. She examined the tools. "And just look at these cunning daisies on the handles." She didn't sound as if she thought they were cunning at all.

Pokey looked anxiously from her mother to her father. What kind of a birthday present was a tool kit? Her mother didn't think it was much of a present, that was certain. You'd think her father would know better! Pokey was angry at him, even more angry than she was at Gordon, who had bought their mother bath crystals when the bathtub didn't even work right. Gordon was stupid, but her father should have known better.

She glared at him.

"Joke, honey," he said to Pokey's mother. "Just my little joke."

"Very funny, Leonard," she said coolly. She only called him "Leonard" when she was angry.

"Open the other one," he said hastily.

She carefully unwrapped the smaller box, as if she were in no hurry to see what it was. But when she opened the box, her whole face lit up.

"Oh, Len, it's beautiful!"

Pokey breathed a deep sigh of relief as her mother held up a gold watch on a chain. It *was* beautiful. The dial had Roman numerals in gold, and the back of the watch was all gold with a swirly design. Mrs. Bloom put it on and smiled broadly.

"Let's eat," Mr. Bloom said. "Everything will be cold by now."

"Oh, who cares!" Mrs. Bloom said. She fingered the watch chain and looked around at all of them, a big smile warming her face.

"I care," Pokey's father retorted. "I'm the one who spent all day slaving over a hot stove."

The dinner turned out perfectly, even though Gordon refused to eat the roast beef because he was still a vegetarian. Pokey's cake, lit with the one candle because her father didn't think her mother would be all that crazy to see thirty-eight candles cluttering up the frosting, was delicious.

"You mean you did this all by yourself?" her mother marveled. "No one helped?"

"It was easy," Pokey said modestly. "You've showed me how lots of times. And besides, all I had to do, really, was read the directions."

"Well, I think it's wonderful," her mother said. "And this is the best birthday I've ever had."

They all laughed, even Gordon.

Mrs. Bloom said that every year.

4

POKEY woke up very early Sunday morning. The house was quiet, and Pokey realized she was the only one who wasn't still asleep.

Her Happy Days Greeting Cards were on her desk, where she'd put them yesterday. Pokey hopped out of bed and got dressed as fast and as quietly as she could.

Today was the day she was going to start winning her transistor radio. She couldn't wait to get going.

She gathered up the greeting cards and order forms and tiptoed down the stairs. She glanced at the kitchen clock. It was only seven-thirty. Pokey frowned. It was much too early to go around ringing doorbells. On Sunday mornings people slept late.

She'd better wait a while.

Pokey tapped her foot impatiently. The second hand of the clock took forever to go around. Seven-thirty-two.

50

Breakfast, she thought. I'll get some breakfast, and maybe by that time it'll be late enough to start.

She took some corn flakes and milk and a banana, and sat down at the kitchen table. She tried to eat as slowly as she could, but she was finished with her breakfast by seven-thirty-seven.

Pokey sighed. At this rate, it would take *years* to earn her transistor radio.

I should practice, Pokey thought suddenly. I can't just go out there and expect to sell things without even knowing what I'm going to say. I have to have a — a sales pitch. That's it, a sales pitch.

She took the box of cards and went into the bathroom. She stood in front of the mirror.

"Madame," she whispered hoarsely, so no one would hear her, "I have here one of the loveliest selections of cards —"

No, that was no good. The cards weren't *that* lovely. She really ought to stress how handy it was to have cards around when you needed them.

"Madame," she said, raising her voice a little; after all, no one could hear her all the way upstairs, and she wanted to know how she sounded as she made her sales pitch.

"Madame, have you ever had to go to a birthday party and suddenly discovered you didn't have a birthday card in the house?"

Pokey shook her head. No, that was no good either. Grown-ups didn't go to birthday parties. Kids did. It was a good idea, but it still wasn't quite right.

Pokey cleared her throat. "My name is Charlotte Bloom and I'm trying to win a transistor radio."

No, no, no! Pokey thought impatiently. That wouldn't do at all. Why should some stranger care whether or not she sold enough cards to win a radio? She had to point out why her customers should want to *buy* Happy Days Greeting Cards, not why she wanted to *sell* them.

"Madame," she began again, "are you one of those people who never has a birthday card around when you need one?"

Oh, that's good, Pokey thought. Then the customer has to talk to you right away.

"Why, yes," Pokey answered herself. "How did you know?"

"Well," she went on, more firmly, "I was like that myself until I discovered Happy Days Greeting Cards. Now I always have a box around the house for unexpected birthdays, and sicknesses and things. Let me show you some of my samples."

Pokey opened the box and held out a card toward her image in the mirror.

"Now, these come in boxes of ten cards, and there's a card for every occasion. Think of how convenient it

52

would be not to have to run out to the store every time someone had a birthday. Or got sick. Or something."

"Well, yes," agreed Pokey, playing the part of her customer again, "that's true."

"And these cards are a real bargain," she went on. "A box costs only a dollar fifty, and when you buy a card in the store, it can be thirty-five or fifty cents. So you can see, ten cards for a dollar fifty is only —"

Pokey stopped to do a quick division problem in her head.

"Fifteen cents a card," she finished. She held out the box.

"Now, that's a real savings."

She nodded at herself in the mirror. That was very good, she thought. If she were a customer, she'd certainly want at least one box. Maybe two, just to make sure she wouldn't run out.

Pokey went back into the kitchen. Now that she knew what she was going to say, she was ready to get started.

But it was still only five minutes to eight.

Would it *never* get any later? Pokey sighed. There wasn't a thing she wanted to do but go out and sell her cards, and here the minutes were going by so slowly —

Suddenly Pokey remembered the cake mix contest. The ten-thousand-dollar grand prize, just for saying why you liked Redimix cakes.

She searched through the kitchen drawer where she had stuck the entry blank the day before and then got herself a piece of paper and a pencil from the telephone table.

"I use Redimix cakes mixes because . . ." Pokey bit her lip. She couldn't just say because they were easy; that was true, but it wasn't good enough to win ten thousand dollars. Everyone would say that. She had to think of something original, clever or different.

"I use Redimix cake mixes because they're so easy even a child can make a beautiful cake."

Pokey shook her head and crossed out the sentence. It was less than twenty-five words, and it was true, but it certainly wasn't good enough to win ten thousand dollars.

Pokey doodled on the edge of her paper. She bit the pencil eraser, and rubbed her forehead with her knuckles.

"I use Redimix cake mixes because even though I'm only a child, I could make my mother a beautiful birthday cake without having to ask her to help me."

That was only twenty-four words, but it sounded silly. Of course she wouldn't ask her mother to help her make her own birthday cake!

Now, think, she ordered herself.

Pokey crossed out sentence after sentence. She had to get two more pieces of paper from the hall table.

54

Finally she sat back and looked at her creation with satisfaction.

That's it, she thought proudly. That's my sentence.

She heaved a deep sigh. It was hard work, thinking up something original and different. She wasn't sure it was original and different enough to win ten thousand dollars, but it was her very best effort and she thought it was pretty good.

Pokey copied her sentence carefully on the entry blank, then addressed the envelope and put a stamp on it.

She looked up at the clock.

It was nine already! Time certainly sped by when she wasn't watching the second hand go around and around.

Now she could go and mail her contest entry, and then maybe it would be late enough to start selling her cards.

She let herself out of the house, being careful to close the door softly behind her. She left her cards on the porch and walked down to the mailbox. She dropped her letter in.

She closed her eyes tightly, crossed all her fingers and both arms, and chanted, "I wish I have good luck. I wish I have good luck."

Her heart began to thump excitedly, almost as if she had already won the ten thousand dollars. She opened her eyes and uncrossed everything. It was silly to get excited so soon. Now calm down, she told herself firmly.

She walked back to the house.

George was sitting on the Blooms' porch rocker, looking through the box of cards.

"Hey, Pokey, what's this for?" he asked.

"Put that down, George," she snapped. "I'm going to sell cards, and those are my samples. You leave them alone. I don't want them all messed up."

"I'm not messing them up!" he said. "I'm just looking at them. Who you going to sell them to?"

"People," she said impatiently. "Whoever wants to buy them." She snatched the box away from him.

"My mother might buy some," George said. "She likes cards."

"Is your mother up yet?" Pokey asked eagerly. It would be a good idea to start with someone she knew; it would be easier to talk to Mrs. Fisher than to a stranger.

"Sure. She gets up real early."

George led Pokey around to his back door, and she followed him into the kitchen. Mrs. Fisher was in her bathrobe, drinking coffee, and Mr. Fisher was looking sleepily down at a plate of eggs.

"Hello, Pokey," George's mother said. "You're out bright and early this morning."

"Hi, Mrs. Fisher," Pokey said nervously. She hesitated a moment. Should she use her sales pitch, or would it sound funny? It was really supposed to be said at someone's front door, to a stranger; maybe it wouldn't be the right thing to say to a neighbor in the middle of breakfast.

Oh, well, Pokey thought, I have to practice it the way I'd say it with everybody else, otherwise what's the point of practicing?

"Are you one of those people," she began briskly, "who never has a birthday card around when you need one?"

Mrs. Fisher smiled. George's father looked up from his eggs and gazed blankly at Pokey.

"I never thought much about it," Mrs. Fisher said.

Pokey groaned inwardly. That wasn't what she was supposed to say!

"But I guess I am," Mrs. Fisher added with a smile.

Pokey sighed with relief.

"So was I," she went on more confidently, "until I discovered Happy Days Greeting Cards. Now I always have a birthday card around when I need one. Or an anniversary card. Or whatever."

She held the box out to Mrs. Fisher, then snatched it back again. That wasn't the way she had rehearsed it. She opened the box, and pulled out a card.

"Now, here is one of the Happy Days cards. They come in a box of ten, and there's a card for every occasion."

Mrs. Fisher looked at the card and grinned. She passed it to her husband, who stared at it wordlessly, and handed it back.

"Well, they certainly do have a card for every occa-

sion," said Mrs. Fisher, giving the card back to Pokey. Pokey looked down at it. It said, in flowery script:

To Great-Grandmother,

on Hallowe'en.

Pokey frowned. She didn't know how many people would need a Hollowe'en card for their great-grandmother. She'd better hurry and point out what a bargain the cards were.

"You know, Mrs. Fisher, a card like this could easily cost you thirty-five or fifty cents at the store."

"Wouldn't buy a card like that at the store," Mr. Fisher mumbled.

Pokey felt nervous again. She was not convincing them that they needed her product. This wasn't a good start at all.

"And there are ten cards to a box, and it's fifty — I mean, a dollar fifty for a box of fifteen — no, ten, I mean — so you can see that's a real bargain."

Oh, that was terrible! Pokey thought miserably. How could I get mixed up like that, after I practiced?

Suddenly she didn't know what to say next. She just stood there, clutching the box of cards against her chest, and staring at Mr. Fisher, who was glumly munching a piece of toast.

"It must be very convenient to have cards around when you need them," George's mother remarked.

I was supposed to say that! Pokey realized unhappily. *I'm* the salesman! What a terrible salesman I am!

Pokey felt as if she were going to cry. She'd really made a mess of her first customer; and what if this happened every time she rang a doorbell? She'd never sell anybody anything. The whole idea had been stupid. What made her think she could sell enough to earn a pencil, let alone a radio?

"I'll take a box, Pokey," said Mrs. Fisher.

"You will? Oh, that's great!" Pokey bubbled. She couldn't believe it! She ripped an order form from her pad, and scrawled Mrs. Fisher's name and address on it. She tore off the little receipt at the bottom of the order blank and handed it to George's mother.

"Do you want the money now?" she asked Pokey.

"Yes please. I have to send it in with the order."

Pokey danced from foot to foot as Mrs. Fisher got her purse and pulled a dollar and two quarters from her wallet.

She'd made a sale! She'd made her very first sale on her very first try!

Maybe she wasn't so terrible a salesman after all!

George followed her out of his house and down the sidewalk.

"I told you she'd buy some," he said cheerfully. Pokey practically skipped down the street.

"Where are you going now?" he asked, running to catch up with her.

"Down the block," she said. "To sell more cards."

"Can I watch?" he asked.

"No, George, you better go home. This is business, you know."

"That's not fair!" he protested. "I gave you some business. I might be able to help you some more."

"Well," Pokey hesitated. She really didn't want George tagging along, but it was true that he'd given her her first opportunity to make a sale. It would be mean to tell him he couldn't go with her.

"Well," she said, "maybe you could be my assistant."

"Oh, yeah!" George said eagerly. "I'll do that. What do I have to do?"

"You carry the box of cards and my order form and pencil," she said. "And when I hold out my hand, you give them to me. I'll say, 'Cards, George,' and you hand me the cards."

"And when do I give you this?" he asked, looking at the pad of order blanks.

"When I say, 'Order forms,' you give that to me, and the pencil too. Understand?"

"Roger," George said snappily.

61

Mr. Graham, Pokey's next-door neighbor, was already out mowing his lawn, so Pokey knew it wasn't too early to ring his doorbell.

Mrs. Graham opened the door and smiled. "Hello, Pokey. Hello, George."

Pokey plunged right in.

"Are you one of those people who never have a birthday card when you need one?"

Mrs. Graham smiled sympathetically. "No, dear. I have boxes and boxes of them in the coat closet. My grandson sells them, and we had to buy enough so that he could get a pocket knife."

"Oh," Pokey said dejectedly. All the excitement and confidence drained out of her, like a limp balloon after a pin has been thrust into it.

"I'm sorry, dear. But I just don't have room for any more boxes up there."

"Okay," Pokey sighed. She turned to go, and Mrs. Graham gently closed the door.

George followed her down the steps and across the street. She would try the Millers next. She knew them too.

Donny Miller answered the door. He was six.

"Is your mother home?" Pokey asked.

"Ma!" Donny shrieked. "Pokey wants ya!"

"What is it?" Mrs. Miller called.

"I don't know!" Donny yelled back.

"I'm selling greeting cards." This was no way to make a sale, Pokey thought glumly. She couldn't very well scream out her sales pitch for Mrs. Miller to hear at the other end of the house.

"She's selling cards," Donny yelled.

"No thank you," Mrs. Miller called back.

"She says no," Donny reported, and slammed the door shut.

Pokey sighed and trudged down the steps.

"We're not doing too well, huh, Pokey?" George said.

"Well," Pokey replied, trying not to feel discouraged, "we just started. We have to expect this kind of thing. There are lots more people to try."

Pokey rang the Sterns' doorbell. Mrs. Stern answered the door in her bathrobe. She looked sleepy and irritable. Pokey hoped she hadn't woken her up — that certainly wouldn't put her customer in a good mood.

"Are you one of those people who never have a greeting card around when you need one?" Pokey began.

Mrs. Stern laughed sharply. "No," she said, "but my husband is."

Puzzled, Pokey didn't know what to say next.

"Today happens to be our anniversary," Mrs. Stern went on loudly. She turned her head to look over her shoulder. "Do you think anyone remembered?" she said. "Do you think anyone sent me so much as a card?" She was practically shouting.

"Happy anniversary, Mrs. Stern," George said suddenly.

She looked down at him, seeing him next to Pokey as if she'd just now noticed him.

"Thank you, dear," she said. "You're the only person who said that to me today."

"How many years anniversary is it?" he asked curiously.

"Plenty, dear," she sighed. "Plenty of years."

Pokey felt she was losing control of the situation. Her customer was getting distracted.

"Maybe if Mr. Stern had a box of Happy Days Greeting Cards around the house in some convenient place," she suggested, "he would remember important events, like birthdays or anniversaries."

"Birthdays!" Mrs. Stern snorted. "In twenty-six years he hasn't remembered a birthday."

"And these cards are a real bargain," Pokey went on desperately. "Why, you'd pay thirty-five or fifty cents for cards like these in the store —"

"Not that cheapskate," Mrs. Stern bellowed. "He wouldn't pay thirty-five cents for his wife's birthday even if he *did* remember it."

"But here are ten cards for a dollar fifty," Pokey babbled heedlessly, "which is only fifteen cents a card, so it's really cheap."

"Cheap enough for a cheapskate," George added, sounding very pleased at his own cleverness.

"Maybe you got something there," Mrs. Stern said, rumpling George's hair fondly. "Cheap enough for a cheapskate. You wait; I'll get the money."

She closed the door.

Pokey turned on him furiously.

"You shouldn't have said that!" she hissed.

"Why not. She's buying the cards, isn't she?"

"But you shouldn't have called Mr. Stern a cheapskate," Pokey insisted.

"That's what *she* called him," George said stubbornly.

"Well, she can call him that; she's married to him. But you —"

The door opened and Mrs. Stern held out two dollar bills.

Pokey gave her fifty cents' change.

"Order forms, George," she snapped.

George handed her the pad and pencil.

"Roger," he said smartly.

Pokey wrote out Mrs. Stern's order and handed her the receipt.

"I'll deliver them as soon as I get them from the company," Pokey promised.

"Well, I hope it's soon," Mrs. Stern said loudly. "Somebody around here is having a birthday next month."

"Thank you, Mrs. Stern," Pokey said. "Let's go, George."

"Roger," George replied, and turned on his heel. He marched down the steps.

"I'm a good assistant, aren't I?" he asked.

"You're doing okay. But listen, George, I didn't tell you to talk to the customers. You leave that to me. From now on, just keep quiet."

George shook his head. "I still think she liked it when I called him a cheapskate. I bet she wouldn't have bought the cards if I wasn't there."

Pokey didn't answer. She had the uncomfortable feeling that George might be right.

By eleven o'clock, Pokey was convinced that her first two sales had been beginner's luck. She and George had been at every house from their own block clear on up to Providence Place and back down again. She hadn't sold another box of cards all morning.

By the time they got back to Pokey's house, her feet hurt and her shoulders slumped.

"We could try again after lunch," George suggested. He didn't seem tired at all.

"We'll see," Pokey said dully. She dragged herself up the front steps to the porch. Maybe she wouldn't have felt so exhausted if all those doors hadn't been slammed in her face, but being turned down time after

66

time was discouraging enough to make her lose all confidence in her salesmanship.

She went into the house.

"Charlotte? Is that you?" her mother called. "Where have you *been?*"

Pokey went slowly into the kitchen. Her parents were sitting at the table with the Sunday papers spread out between them. Gordon was standing over the blender, pouring things into the glass container.

"I've been selling greeting cards," Pokey sighed, and slumped down on a chair.

"Well," her father said, surprised. "When did that start?"

"Just today. I didn't do too well. I wanted to sell enough to get a transistor radio. But I only sold two boxes."

"How many do you have to sell to get the radio?" her mother asked.

"Forty-four boxes."

Gordon gave a short, nasty laugh and turned on the blender.

"I'll buy a box," her mother shouted over the racket the blender made.

"Oh, you don't have to," Pokey said. She was sure her mother felt sorry for her, and was just buying a box out of pity.

"But I want to," her mother insisted. "You know I

never have a card around when I need one. How much does a box cost?"

"A dollar fifty."

"That's very reasonable," her mother shouted.

Gordon turned off the blender and poured his drink into a glass.

"What *is* that you're drinking?" his father asked.

"It's a healthshake," Gordon said. "A mixture of all natural ingredients."

"Like what, for instance?" asked Mr. Bloom.

"Applesauce, banana, milk, wheat germ, brewer's yeast —"

"Yeast?" Mrs. Bloom echoed.

"Where does it get the pink color?" his father asked. "Did you put food coloring in it?"

"Food coloring!" Gordon shrieked. "I just told you this was all natural ingredients. The pink is from the beets."

"Oh, my God," Mr. Bloom said weakly.

Pokey put her hand over her mouth and rolled her eyes.

"Listen, you don't even know what it tastes like," Gordon said irritably. "And it's good for you. You ought to try it. Builds strong muscles, teeth and bones, Nature's way."

"Puts hair on your chest," his father added.

"Just what I need," murmured Mrs. Bloom.

Gordon stalked out of the kitchen with his glass, and they heard the closet door slam.

"There he goes again," Pokey commented. "Why does he have to lock himself in the closet every time he uses the phone?"

"I guess he likes privacy," her mother said.

"Did it ever occur to you," Mr. Bloom said darkly, "that he might just like closets?"

5

BY THURSDAY, Pokey had to admit to herself that selling enough greeting cards to win a transistor radio was a lot harder than she'd expected.

She'd thought she'd just have to knock on doors, give her sales pitch, and take down the orders. She'd never imagined that she would go from door to door and be turned away almost everywhere she went. But, by the end of the week, her afternoons had blurred into a sameness of "No thank yous" and slammed doors.

I might as well face it, Pokey told herself. It isn't just hard — it's impossible. She didn't know how the Fuller Brush men did it. Maybe some people were born salesmen. Maybe some people just didn't get discouraged, no matter how many times they heard, "No thank you" — or worse.

But me, Pokey thought; I wasn't cut out to be a salesman.

Sadly, she slipped the six orders she'd managed to get into the Happy Days envelope. She hadn't even sold enough to earn the simulated 14K gold heart-shaped locket — even if she'd wanted it. That was ten boxes. If you sold less than ten boxes, you only made ten cents a box. She'd worked almost all week for sixty cents.

Pokey sighed, and took out her notebook. She had math homework to do, and since she already felt miserable anyway, she might as well get it over with.

She started on the first problem, but her mind wandered. She kept thinking about the transistor radio she wasn't going to win.

Maybe, thought Pokey, a little music would help me concentrate. She went up to Gordon's room; the door was open and Gordon wasn't there, so Pokey borrowed his radio and took it back to her room.

She turned it on.

"And don't touch that dial," a voice blared, "because coming up next is our guest, Virginia Hopewell, who's going to tell you how she won fabulous prizes in every contest she ever entered!"

Pokey snapped her math book shut and adjusted the volume on the radio. To win every contest you ever entered! That seemed impossible — but here was a woman who said she did it.

"And now for our guest, Virginia Hopewell. Virginia, this sounds incredible. Did you really win prizes in every contest you ever entered?"

"Yes, Brad, I did. Once I discovered the Secret."

Pokey leaned forward in her chair and stared intently at the radio, as if there were a picture coming from it as well as sound.

"Wow, that's kind of hard to believe, isn't it?" the announcer went on.

"That's just it, Brad," Miss Hopewell said. "That's the key to the whole thing. *Believing* it's possible."

"You mean, that's the Secret?"

"That's the Secret. Once I learned that, there was no stopping me. My belief in myself was so strong I just couldn't lose."

Pokey frowned.

"Come now, Virginia, there's got to be more to it than that. You're saying, aren't you, that wishing makes it so?"

"But it's true, Brad. Wishing *does* make it so. You just have to know how to wish properly."

Pokey shook her head. This was very confusing. She'd wished for a lot of things, and an awful lot of her wishes hadn't come true. She never knew that there was a right way and a wrong way to do your wishing.

"Then there's a trick to it," the announcer continued. "A certain method you have to use."

"Why, of course," Miss Hopewell said. "The trick

is to visualize yourself winning the prize you want. When I entered my first contest, the prize I wanted was an outboard motorboat. Well, I didn't just wish for that boat. I concentrated all my thoughts on owning it. I pictured myself in the boat, on the water, I planned where I was going to keep it in the winter — I even went out and bought life preservers for it. And I didn't just do this once — I did it every day for weeks. At least three times a day I pictured myself in that boat. I never let myself think that I might not win it. The concentrated energy of my mind power brought me that boat."

"Well, Virginia, that sounds fantastic."

Pokey agreed. It sounded impossible. It was too easy. What if everybody listening to the radio entered the same contest? What if they all concentrated on winning the same prize? They couldn't all win it, could they?

But still . . . maybe the person with the strongest mind power would win. Then what about all the other people who had wished three times a day? I wouldn't work for them, so that must mean it didn't work.

"And speaking of contests, friends, let's not forget our own Radio 55 WRBG Jackpot Jubilee. Three times a day we pick a card from our giant barrel and call someone out there. If they can tell us how much is in our Jackpot, they win the whole thing. If they can't, we add five dollars and fifty-five cents to the Jackpot. Right now there's five hundred and forty-nine dollars and forty-five cents in that Jackpot, and you could be the lucky winner. Just send a postcard with your name, address and telephone number to —"

Pokey ripped a piece of paper from her notebook and copied down the address.

"And now, if you want to talk to Virginia on the telephone, why not give us a call at 755–5555. The lines are open, and she's waiting to talk to you."

Pokey jumped up and ran to the phone in her parents' bedroom. She would talk to this woman, and ask her that question about everybody wishing for the same prize. Maybe Miss Hopewell could explain it to her.

The line was busy. Pokey dialed again. The line was still busy. She ran back to her room and got the radio, so she wouldn't miss anything, and flopped down on her parents' bed with the radio and the phone.

She had to get through to Miss Hopewell. She had to find out if this Secret really worked.

Pokey dialed again and again until her fingers began to get sore. Every time she dialed, the harsh buzz of the busy signal greeted her.

And then, finally, Pokey heard a click, and the phone was ringing at the other end. She couldn't believe it. Maybe she had dialed wrong. Maybe she was calling the wrong number.

It seemed as if she had been holding on forever when the ringing stopped and a woman's voice asked, "Do you want to speak to Brad's guest?"

"Yes," Pokey whispered. Her hand began to tremble.

"All right; he'll be with you in a couple of minutes. Just turn your radio off when you hear him talking to you."

"Okay," Pokey said hoarsely.

Her heart began to thump as she waited. She was too excited to listen to what was being said on the radio. Suddenly a deep voice boomed in her ear.

"WRBG Radio fifty-five — Where Radio Begins. Hi, there, how are you today?"

Pokey clutched the phone to her ear. "Fine thank you," she whispered.

"Turn your radio down and your voice up, please," Brad said cheerfully.

"Okay." She turned off the radio.

"Did you have a question for Virginia?"

"Yes," Pokey said, louder.

"Go ahead. She's listening."

"I wanted to know —" Pokey's mind went blank.

What had she wanted to know? She couldn't remember! She couldn't think of a thing to say!

"Don't be nervous," the announcer soothed. "Just pretend you're talking to a friend on the phone."

"Okay." Pokey gulped.

"Now, what was your question?"

"My question was —" Pokey frantically searched for something to say. This was awful! He would hang up on her in a minute, and she'd never find out how all those people could win the same prize.

That was it! Pokey let out a deep sigh of relief.

"What if everybody enters the same contest?" she asked, her voice louder and firmer now. "What if they all concentrate on winning the first prize? They can't *all* win."

"A good question, young lady." Pokey felt a little flash of pride. "How about that, Virginia?"

"Well, of course they're not all going to win the first prize," Miss Hopewell said over the phone. "You see, it's not really that easy to maintain your concentration over a long period of time. Sometimes a contest will run for months, and it's very difficult to focus your mind's energy on that prize three times a day, every day, for several months. People forget. They do it for a while, and then stop, or only do it occasionally, when they remember to. But one person is going to keep up that level of concentration every single day until the contest is over, and that's the person who's going to win the prize he wants."

"Does that answer your question?" the announcer asked.

"I guess so," Pokey said doubtfully.

"Thanks for the call," he said, and hung up.

Pokey put the receiver back on the hook and took the radio into her room again. She sat down at her desk and rested her chin on her hands.

The person who concentrated hardest was the person who was going to win. It wasn't easy, Miss Hopewell had said. But it sounded easy. It couldn't take very long, just a couple of minutes a day, to picture yourself with your prize. Why should people find that too hard?

Pokey closed her eyes. She tried to picture herself winning the Redimix contest. She saw piles of money tied together with rubber bands. She was giving some of the money to her mother, and keeping the rest of it for herself, in her desk drawer. No, she was putting it in a safe, so no one could steal it.

We don't have a safe, Pokey thought suddenly. Oh, well, with ten thousand dollars I can afford to buy one to keep the money in.

She pictured herself going to the store and buying a transistor radio. It had an earplug, and everything.

She imagined counting out the money. One thousand, two thousand, three thousand — the bills were piling up on her desk.

This isn't hard, Pokey thought.

She opened her eyes. There, she said to herself. That's one time I thought about it today. Now, I only have to do that twice more.

Then she remembered the POW All-Purpose Spray Cleaner dream house contest. She'd have to concentrate on that, too.

Pokey closed her eyes again. She saw herself walking through the door of her dream house. Oh, no good! That wasn't her dream house she was imagining. That was her own door, on her own house.

She shook her head, as if to clear her mind. Try again.

She imagined a castle, with high towers and a moat, perched on the top of a craggy mountain.

That's silly! She told herself sternly. I don't want a castle! *Concentrate.*

Finally she got a picture of a very modern, one-story house, with lots of big picture windows, and some stone and redwood siding. There was a great, rolling lawn in the front, and a light post with a sign hanging from it, which read *the blooms* in very plain letters with no capitals.

Inside the house everything was new. Pokey pictured triangular bathtubs, with every faucet gleaming and not one of them leaking. All the drains worked perfectly.

She pictured her own room — the one with the Ping-Pong table and the color television set. She saw herself behind the counter of her soda fountain, making thick shakes for Nora and Bethanne. Oh, what a beautiful picture it was!

She pictured Gordon's room. It had bars across it. It locked from the *out*side. It was in the basement — dank and musty. She pictured Gordon inside, hands grasping the iron bars, yelling for her to let him out. There was no phone in the room, and no closet.

That's not very nice, she told herself sternly. That's really a mean way to think about your own brother.

But she grinned anyway. It was *her* imagining — and she could think up anything she wanted.

Pokey opened her eyes and took a deep breath. There — that took care of that for now.

Was there anything else? Pokey thought for a moment and then remembered the Brewmaster's Black Forest Bock Beer Sweepstakes. The grand prize was a dune buggy.

Pokey closed her eyes again. She pictured a dune buggy. She got in and —

She opened her eys. She didn't know how to drive a dune buggy. She didn't know how to drive *anything*. How could she concentrate on a picture of herself scooting around in a dune buggy if she didn't know the first thing about how it worked?

Ah, Pokey breathed, that's it. She closed her eyes again, and pictured herself in the dune buggy on the passenger's side. Her father was in the driver's seat and they were chugging along the beach, zipping over dunes —

Could a dune buggy really drive over sand dunes? Pokey wasn't sure. After all, sand dunes were made of sand, and a dune buggy would be pretty heavy. All the sand might squish down, and they could be trapped in the middle of the dune, buried in piles of sand.

But why would it be called a dune buggy if it couldn't drive over dunes? That didn't make sense. Then it would be a beach buggy, or a sand buggy, not a dune buggy.

You're not concentrating, Pokey scolded herself. What difference does it make if it drives over dunes or just sand? It still would be a neat thing to have.

"Gordon! Charlotte! Come on down — time for dinner!"

"Coming!" Pokey called.

She got up from her chair and stretched; all that concentrating had made her muscles stiff.

Her eye fell on the math book, closed, untouched, on the desk where she'd left it.

Rats, she thought, now I'll have to do my homework after dinner and miss television.

Well, maybe it would be worth it.

After all, what were a couple of missed television shows compared to ten thousand dollars, her dream house, and a dune buggy?

6

Ow!" Pokey yelled, as Bethanne jabbed her in the back with her fingers. The picture of her dream house dissolved. Pokey looked around guiltily. The whole class was giggling. Mr. Nader fixed his stern gaze on her face.

"Since the thought of telling us what plankton is seems to give Charlotte a pain, maybe someone else can enlighten us."

Tina Wirth's hand shot up.

I know what plankton is, Pokey thought angrily. That isn't fair. He didn't even give me a chance. Just because I didn't hear the question —

But, Pokey had to admit, there had been a *lot* of questions she hadn't heard in the past week. After the first couple of days of concentrating on a regular schedule (first thing in the morning, as soon as she came home from school, and just before she went to bed), Pokey began to forget once in a while. Virginia Hopewell had been right. It wasn't that easy to concentrate; it wasn't even that easy to *remember* to concentrate.

So she began to do her concentrating whenever she happened to remember it. Since the morning was always such a rush, Pokey was constantly forgetting her first-thing-in-the-morning concentrating. And then she seemed to remember she'd forgotten it at the most inconvenient times — like during math or science. She knew she ought to pay attention; and Mr. Nader was getting angrier and angrier at her each time he called on her and she didn't know what he was talking about. But she couldn't take the chance of forgetting again. It was important to keep her concentrated mind power at a higher pitch than any of the other millions of contestants who might also be trying to wish themselves a dune buggy or a dream house or ten thousand dollars.

And now there was the WRBG Jackpot Jubilee to concentrate on too, and the Old Hickory Cigars Cadillac Contest, so her imagining took quite a bit of time.

"Pokey," Bethanne said firmly as they finished up their lunch, "if you don't stop sleeping in school, you're going to be in big trouble."

"I'm not sleeping!" Pokey said indignantly.

"Well, it sure looks like you're sleeping," Bethanne

retorted. "It practically takes an alarm clock to wake you up."

"Maybe somebody hypnotized you," Nora suggested nervously, "and you get into these trances whenever somebody says 'bananas' or something."

"What *are* you talking about?" demanded Bethanne.

"Well, on Terror Theater last night this man got hypnotized; before he was hypnotized, he was really okay, but afterwards whenever he heard the name 'Sheldon' he turned into a crazed maniac with a lust to kill."

Bethanne snorted.

"I don't have a lust to kill," Pokey said. "Whatever that means. I've just been concentrating."

"Concentrating!" Bethanne shrieked. "You've been dreaming."

"Well, sort of," Pokey admitted. "I'm kind of concentrating on dreaming."

"Speaking of crazed maniacs," Bethanne remarked to Nora.

"There was this woman on the radio," Pokey explained, "who said if you entered a contest and wished hard enough, you could win any prize you wanted."

"Oh, sure," Bethanne said sarcastically. "Santa Claus brings it."

"Well, she said she's won every contest she ever entered."

85

"Do you believe it?" asked Nora curiously.

"Why should she lie?" Pokey asked. "Why would they let her be on the radio if it wasn't true?"

"So what has that got to do with your dreaming?"

"I'm supposed to picture the prize I want and imagine myself having it. I have to do it every day, three times."

"You don't have to do it in school, do you?" asked Nora.

"But I keep forgetting, and then I have to do it when I remember," Pokey explained.

"You keep this up," Bethanne warned, "and you'll be the richest left-back kid in class."

"I know," Pokey sighed.

"Now, listen," Bethanne said, dismissing Pokey's problems. "I absolutely have everybody's word that they can make it this Saturday."

"Make what?" asked Pokey blankly.

"You mean you've forgotten?" Bethanne wailed.

"The bike hike," Nora reminded her. "To clean up the lot."

"Oh," Pokey nodded, "oh yeah. No, I didn't forget."

But she had. She'd been looking forward to it so much at first, and then it got postponed week after week, and finally she'd just stopped looking forward to it. She'd stopped thinking about it at all.

86

"Hey, that's great!" she exclaimed. "I can't believe we're really going to do it at last."

"Well, we are," Bethanne declared. "I just hope that lot is still filthy."

"Oh, I'm sure it is," Pokey said encouragingly.

"We'll all meet at my house at ten," Bethanne ordered. "Don't be late."

Howard Fell and Tony Murch came strolling toward their table. Tony gave Howard a push, and he staggered into Pokey's chair, knocking her against Nora.

"Hey, cut that out!" Pokey cried. She pushed Howard away and glared at Tony.

"We heard you were finally going to do it this Saturday," Tony said. "Don't you think your mommies will be angry when you get yourselves all dir-ty?"

Bethanne and Pokey exchanged disgusted glances.

"Anthony," Bethanne said icily, "go play with your blocks."

Tony looked at Howard and sniffled dramatically. "We aren't wanted here, Howard."

"You noticed," Bethanne said. "How smart of you."

"And I'll bet they don't want us to help them clean up the garbage, either," Tony went on.

Bethanne stood up angrily.

"You better not help us," she warned. "You just better not make trouble."

"What will you do?" Tony sneered. "Tell your mommy?"

"Oh, great," Bethanne scowled as the boys walked away. "That's all we need, those two."

"What dopes," Pokey muttered. "They'll spoil everything."

"No they won't," Bethanne promised fervently. "We won't let them."

Who won't? Pokey asked herself glumly. Who was going to stop the biggest, meanest pests in their whole class from doing anything they felt like doing?

After lunch, Pokey told herself firmly there'd be no more concentrating during school hours. She paid close attention to everything that went on in class, and even raised her hand twice to answer questions. She got one math problem wrong when she had to go up and do it on the board, but at least when Mr. Nader called on her, she stood right up without having to have Bethanne jab her in the back.

When she got home from school, her mother was hard at work.

"Oh, hi, honey," she said, looking up from her sketch. "I didn't even hear you come in."

Pokey looked down at the drawing. "Uck."

"Don't you like it?" her mother asked.

"Oh, the drawing is fine. The bug is ucky."

"That's a praying mantis," her mother said.

"I know that. I think it's ucky. I saw a movie once where there were these giant praying mantises and they took over a whole town in Arizona. All you could see were their legs going past the windows of houses, they were so big."

"Well, I'd think they were ucky too, if they grew that big," her mother agreed. "Listen, could you go to the shopping center for me? I need a newsprint pad, and I don't want to stop now to get it. Your brother seems to have disappeared."

"Did you look in the closet?" Pokey suggested.

"Every closet near every phone in the house." Her mother grinned. "He must have gone out. He grunted at me when he came home, and I haven't seen him since."

"Okay," Pokey said. "What kind of pad should I get?"

Mrs. Bloom tore the cover off one of her large pads and handed it to her. "Just match this," she said. "Get me exactly the same kind."

"Can I get myself an Italian ice while I'm there?"

"All right. Take three dollars from my purse," her mother said, already back at work on her mantis.

Pokey took the money and ran downstairs and out the door. She was halfway down the block when George came running up behind her.

"Hey, Pokey, where you going?"

"I have to get a pad for my mother at the art store," she said.

"Okay. I'll come too."

He trotted along beside her.

"We did an experiment today," George announced. "Mrs. King was trying to make this egg go into a bottle and it splattered all over her dress. You should have seen her. It was a real mess."

"We did that in third grade too," Pokey remembered. "I think you're supposed to use a hard-boiled egg."

"Yeah," George agreed. "Boy, was that funny."

George was still chuckling to himself when they got to the shopping center. Pokey went inside the art shop to find her mother's pad, while George waited outside and tried to balance himself on the rim of a planter.

Pokey found the right pad and paid for it. She had enough change left over to buy two Italian ices; she was sure her mother wouldn't mind if she bought one for George. She couldn't very well eat her own and watch him staring at her hungrily with every lick she took.

Pokey got cherry flavor and George got root beer. As they walked slowly through the mall, Pokey suddenly remembered that she hadn't done her concentrating since the morning.

"Wait a minute, George," she said, stopping short.

She closed her eyes, and pictured her dream house. At least, now that she knew what it looked like, it was easier to start right in imagining, without castles and teepees and things cluttering up her mind first.

"What are you doing?" asked George. "Are you wishing for good luck again?"

"Shh!" hissed Pokey. "Sort of."

She pictured the bathtubs, her beautiful room with the soda fountain —

"Well, if it isn't Miss Garbage of 1999!" somebody crowed, and pushed the back of her head so hard that her nose and mouth went straight into her Italian ice.

Pokey shrieked and whirled around, cherry ice smeared across her face. She sputtered in rage, and Howard Fell clutched his sides, laughing.

"Rudolph the Red-Nosed Reindeer!" he yelled, pointing at her.

"Howard, you rat!" Pokey screamed. She raised her arm and hurled the rest of her Italian ice at him. He ducked, and the cup fell into a large artificial bush.

"You pick that up, you litterbug," Howard squeaked, trying to sound like a little old lady.

"Why don't you get out of here?" George said suddenly, coming up on the other side of Howard.

Howard looked down at him. "I'm not bothering you, am I, shrimp?"

"Don't call me a shrimp," George said. "And leave Pokey alone."

"George," Pokey began. She really wished George would mind his own business.

"Oh, are you her bodyguard?" Howard asked sarcastically. "I didn't recognize you in your midget disguise."

"Let's go, George," Pokey said, wiping her face with the paper bag the pad had been in.

"See you at the dump," Howard said cheerfully, waving at her as she walked away.

"You'll be right at home there," Pokey called back. "With the rest of the garbage."

"Oh, yeah?" Howard retorted. Pokey and George kept on walking. George looked back over his shoulder at Howard. "You want to make something of it?" he yelled.

Howard just laughed.

"What a dope," Pokey muttered.

"Yeah. It's a good thing I came along, huh?" George said importantly.

Pokey grinned to herself. "Oh, sure," she agreed.

"He better not start up with you when *I'm* around," George said threateningly.

"Right," Pokey said. She could hardly keep from giggling, but she knew George would be very hurt if she

92

did, so she tightened her lips and bit them to hold the laughter in.

"Hey, there's Gordon," George said suddenly.

Pokey looked ahead and saw her brother leaning against the window of Hermes' Health Food Heaven.

"Let's watch him," George whispered. He pulled Pokey into the entranceway of a shoe store and peered around the display window. Pokey stood behind him and looked over his head.

Gordon was trying to see inside the health food store without letting anybody notice he was trying to. Every time someone went in or out, he quickly turned away and leaned back against the window, whistling.

"I don't get it," Pokey said. "Why does he hang around here all the time?"

Gordon was staring into the shop again. Just then a girl came out and, before he could turn away, she started to talk to him. Gordon looked down at his feet; he folded his arms, then unfolded them and stuck his hands in his pockets.

The girl went back into the store, and Gordon leaned against the window and clapped his hand to his head.

"What's the matter with him?" Pokey wondered aloud. "Do you think he's sick or something?" Suddenly she was very worried about her brother. He looked so *strange*.

Gordon peered over his shoulder, took a last glance into the store, and hurried away.

"You know what I think?" George said.

"Come on," urged Pokey. "We have to get home."

"I think he's casing the joint."

"What?"

"Casing the joint," repeated George, slowly and distinctly. "I think he's planning a caper."

"George, what are you talking about?" Pokey asked, exasperated.

"Don't you know *anything*?" George said. "That means he's going to rob the store, and has to look

around first to see how he can rob it without getting caught, or anything."

"Gordon?" Pokey exclaimed. "Gordon, rob a store? Are you crazy?"

"I'm not crazy," George said calmly. "He's the one that's acting weird, you said so yourself. And why should he keep going to that store, unless he's casing it?"

"Because he's on a health food kick," Pokey said. "That's all he eats now."

"But he didn't buy anything," George pointed out. "He didn't even go inside."

"That's true," Pokey said thoughtfully. "Oh, I think you watch too much television, George." But Pokey's voice was doubtful, and unpleasant thoughts began to crowd into her mind.

Gordon, a thief? Gordon, a criminal? Was it possible? Had he done it before, or was this his first caper?

Oh, stop it, Pokey told herself. Now I'm beginning to sound like George.

But what could he be doing there? Why was he so interested in seeing the inside of the store, and so careful about not letting people see that he was interested? That certainly seemed suspicious.

But there could be hundreds of perfectly good reasons for Gordon to be doing that.

Like, for instance —

Pokey shook her head. Well, there must be plenty of good reasons, she insisted to herself. I just can't think of any right now, but that doesn't mean there *aren't* any.

Besides, criminals come from broken homes, or have drunken parents, or are poor and need money to feed their children. Gordon isn't like that. We aren't poor, and he doesn't even *have* any children.

"So I think we better keep him under surveillance," George was saying. "For his own good."

"What?" Pokey hadn't been listening to him.

"Keep him under surveillance," George repeated impatiently. "Shadow him. Keep a tail on Gordon. Don't you know what I'm talking about?"

"Yes," Pokey replied, really disturbed now. "I know what you mean. You want to spy on him."

"It's for his own good, Pokey," George declared. "We can stop him before he does anything."

"Why don't we just stop him now?" Pokey suggested. "Tell him we saw him, and say we know what he's up to."

"Oh, no, that won't work. If he knows we're onto him, he'll just be real careful. Criminals are very cunning."

"Stop calling my brother a criminal!" Pokey cried.

"Well, anyhow, if we tell him, he'll just go on and plan another caper, but he'll know we're suspicious, so he'll do it when we're not around. Like after we're in bed, or something."

"I don't know," Pokey said, "I don't think —"

"And besides, we have no evidence," George said. "You need evidence before you can do anything."

Pokey was too confused to think straight. They had reached their corner, and Gordon was just going into the house.

"It's late, George. I have to go in."

"Okay, but don't forget. We shadow him at all times. If you can't get out, call me and I'll go. But, listen," he said, turning back to call after her, "don't you go without me. You never know what might happen."

"All right, George, all right," Pokey agreed.

"So long," he shouted happily. He was humming as he ran up his front steps.

George was going to enjoy playing detective, Pokey thought sadly. To him, the whole thing is like a TV show.

Well, why not?

It wasn't *his* brother who was embarking on a life of crime.

7

S ATURDAY was gray and gloomy. Pokey kept glancing out the window anxiously. It just couldn't rain! Her parents would never let her go on the bike hike if it rained. They would worry about the brakes on her bike and the cars skidding on the wet roads. They would worry about her getting drenched and catching a cold. It just *couldn't* rain.

"It certainly looks like rain," her mother said, as Pokey gobbled down her breakfast.

"It won't rain," Pokey said firmly. "And I have to go now. It's a quarter to ten." She pushed back her chair and jumped up.

"Charlotte," her mother said worriedly, "I'm sure it's going to rain."

"But it's not raining *now*," Pokey said. "You can't make me stay home just because you think it *might* rain."

"Oh, good grief, let her go already," Gordon cut in. "She won't melt. And besides, I don't want her hanging around and pestering me all day."

"Pestering you!" Pokey exclaimed indignantly. "Hanging around! I don't even go near you, if I can help it!"

Gordon was having a party that night, and Pokey thought he was acting like a crazy person. You'd think he was the only boy in the world ever to give a party; Pokey was glad she wasn't going to be around today. She couldn't take too much more of her brother in his obnoxious phase.

"Look, don't forget what we said about riding single file," her mother reminded her. "And walk your bike across the big intersections. Charlotte, are you listening?"

"*Yes,*" Pokey said impatiently. She pulled out a big trash bag from under the sink. Everyone was bringing plastic bags to put the litter in.

"All right, Good-bye, honey. Please be careful."

"I will," Pokey promised.

She ran out to get her bike. She wheeled it out of the garage, tossed the bag into her basket, and hopped on. Right up to the last minute she had been afraid they were going to change their minds and not let her go. But now she was halfway down the block, on her way, and they weren't running after her yelling, "Wait a minute, wait a minute, we made a mistake!"

It was only a few blocks to Bethanne's house, and when she got there most of the girls were already waiting, clustered on the front lawn. Their bikes were parked all over the sidewalk.

Pokey jumped off her bike and knocked down the kickstand.

"Hi!" she called to Bethanne, who was counting heads. "Am I late? Is everyone here?"

"Almost," said Bethanne. "Sandy and Laurel couldn't come, after all. But I wasn't going to start calling it off all over again. We just have to wait for Joanne."

"I hope it doesn't rain," Nora said glumly. "My glasses will get all wet, and I won't be able to see where I'm going."

"Oh, don't worry so much," Tina said scornfully. "You can always take them off."

"Then I *really* won't be able to see where I'm going," Nora muttered.

"Here she comes!" Bethanne yelled, as Joanne pedaled furiously up the block. Joanne leaped off her bike without braking, dropped the bike on the sidewalk, and flung herself on Bethanne's lawn.

"Wheew!" she gasped. "I'm exhausted."

"Exhausted," laughed Steffie Kramer. "We haven't even started yet."

"Yeah, but I had to walk up to the gas station first and get air in my tire. My brother was fooling around on it and got a flat. And then I was sure I was going to be late —" Joanne was panting. She flopped back on the grass.

"Let me catch my breath."

After a few minutes Bethanne said, "Okay, let's go. Everybody follow me, and stay in line. We'll go up Providence Place, then turn onto Pittsburgh Avenue, and ride along that to Mill Road. Anyway, just follow me. I know how to go."

Bethanne mounted her bike and pedaled slowly down the street as the rest of the girls formed a line behind her.

They rode steadily until they got to Pittsburgh Avenue. Traffic was light and the road was wide enough so that the cars gave them plenty of room.

Bethanne turned around and said something to Nora, and Nora yelled back to Pokey, "We're halfway there. Pass it on."

Pokey passed it on to Steffie. She was beginning to feel a little tired. This was a much longer bike ride than she had ever been on, and Pittsburgh Avenue was uphill.

Riding single file it was hard to talk to anyone, because you had to shout to be heard, and to turn around was dangerous because you might crash into the person in front of you. Pokey wished she could ride next to Nora instead of behind her, but it just wasn't safe.

At the corner of Mill Road and Pittsburgh Avenue they stopped and got off their bikes to wait for the light to change.

"We'd better ride on the sidewalk from here on," Bethanne yelled. "There's too much traffic."

Pokey was relieved. It made her a little nervous when cars sped by right next to her, and sometimes she tried to turn around to see where they were when she heard them coming closer, and felt like she might lose her balance and fall off the bike.

On the sidewalk they had just enough room to ride two by two, and Pokey pulled up next to Nora.

"I'm tired," Pokey panted. "Are you?"

"I sure am," Nora agreed. "But we're almost there."

There were only a few blocks to go up Mill Road to the bus garage when it started to drizzle.

"Oh, no," groaned Nora. "Just what I need."

"We're practically there," Pokey said reassuringly. "Look, you can see the buses from here."

"I can't see anything from here," Nora grunted. "My glasses are all misted up."

"Well, just stay next to me," Pokey said. "You'll be okay."

"We made it!" Bethanne announced, raising her hand in triumph as they braked to a stop at the lot.

"Yay," Joanne gasped weakly. The rain was coming down a little harder now, but no one paid any attention to it except Nora, who took off her glasses and stuck them in her pocket.

The lot was just as Nora had promised — a mess. There was a big sign that said NO DUMPING, but in spite of the sign a great many things had been dumped there. The area was strewn with beer cans, soda bottles, soggy newspapers, broken lunchboxes, odd sneakers, and even a couple of old tires.

"Boy, does this place need us," Bethanne said with satisfaction. "Let's get started."

"Look!" Tina shouted suddenly. She pointed toward Mill Road. "What are *they* doing here?"

Coming across the street toward the lot was a group of four boys. They were on bikes, and they weren't riding single file, but were all bunched up together, paying no attention to the cars honking around them.

Pokey recognized Tony Murch and Howard Fell and two other boys from their class.

"Maybe they want to help," Steffie said dubiously.

"Oh, sure," Tina sneered. "They want to make trouble, that's what they want to do. They'll ruin everything."

Pokey knew Tina was right.

The boys sped across Mill Road and came to a screeching stop next to the lot.

"Is this where we sign up for Girls against Garbage?" Tony asked Bethanne.

He dropped his bike, and Bethanne leaped out of the way just in time to prevent the bike from falling on her foot.

"We want to help," he said innocently. "Don't we, guys?"

Alan Foster nodded solemnly. "*Sure* we do."

Howard picked up a sodden mass of newspaper and inspected it. Then he ripped it into a hundred tiny little pieces and flung them over their heads.

"Happy New Year!" he cried, and staggered around, pretending to be drunk.

Pokey looked from the boys to Bethanne, who frowned as she surveyed the situation.

"Okay," Bethanne said suddenly, as if she had just made up her mind, "let's get to work."

8

BETHANNE opened her plastic bag. "If we all spread out and take a different spot, we can get this done really fast." She was going to act as if the boys weren't there.

Pokey took the bag from her bike basket and walked toward the middle of the lot away from the boys. There was plenty to pick up, and she began to collect beer and soda cans and toss them into her bag.

Howard came toward her. He was skipping lightly on his toes and singing.

"Tiptoe through the garbage, through the garbage, through the garbage dump, come tiptoe through the garbage with me. La la la . . ."

Pokey ignored him. She turned her back and continued to clean up her part of the lot. Howard skipped around her and delicately dropped the tiniest piece of torn newspaper into her bag.

"La la la," he hummed, skipping away. Pokey found

an old tattered sneaker and dropped it into the bag. Howard came skipping back, with the remains of a grimy shoelace.

"Look what I found," he said gaily, and tossed it in after the sneaker. "Oh, isn't this fun?"

Pokey clenched her teeth. I'm going to ignore him, she promised herself. He'll get tired of pestering me if I just pay no attention to him.

She walked off and found a pile of old rags. They smelled awful, and she lifted them with the tips of her fingers and tried not to breathe as she dumped them in the trash bag.

Suddenly a flying missile hit Pokey in the back. She whirled around, and Howard called, "Oh, I missed. I was trying to get that in the bag. My, my."

Pokey picked up the beer can that Howard had thrown. She felt herself growing hot with anger. She glanced from the can to Howard, and for a moment she felt a terrible urge to hurl the beer can at his head. After all, she still owed him something for pushing her face into her cherry ice.

But she took a deep breath and reminded herself, *ignore him.* Just ignore him. He'll go away.

Besides, she might miss again.

Pokey pushed her wet hair out of her eyes. It was raining harder now, and her shirt felt clammy and unpleasant against her skin.

She heard the sound of shrill voices off in the dis-

tance, but paid no attention to them. She had to keep blinking the rain out of her eyes, and everything she picked up felt slimy.

"Fight! Fight!"

Pokey straightened up and saw Howard running toward the Carver Street corner of the lot. It was too far away and it was raining too hard for Pokey to see what was happening. A cluster of the girls were screaming and hopping around something.

Pokey flung her bag over her shoulder and ran after Howard. Who was fighting, she wondered.

The bag bounced against her, hitting her in the back, bump, bump, bump, as she ran.

Now she could see what was happening. Tina Wirth was chasing Alan Foster around the shouting group, using her bag to swing at him like a baseball bat. Every once in a while, a blow would land, *thwack!* and Alan would yell.

Just as Pokey ran up to the circle, Frankie Flynn stuck his foot out and tripped Tina. He grabbed the bag away from her as she sprawled on the ground.

"No fair!" Bethanne screamed. "Two against one!"

She lunged at Frankie, trying to snatch the bag away.

Pokey and Nora pulled Tina up. Her shirt was smeared with dirt.

"You creep!" she howled. She shook off Nora and

Pokey's help and tore after Frankie, who was in a tug of war with Bethanne for Tina's trash bag.

She flung herself at him like a football tackle, and sent him tumbling to his knees. Bethanne grabbed the bag away from him.

"Two against one! No fair!" shouted Howard gleefully. Before Pokey realized what was happening, he'd snatched her bag away from her and dumped the trash she'd collected over Bethanne's head.

Bethanne screamed with rage, and Pokey charged after Howard, revenge in her heart.

"You stink, Howard Fell!" she screamed. What a terrible thing to do, dumping garbage on someone's head! And after she had spent half an hour trying to clean up that garbage!

She and Bethanne managed to get Howard trapped between them. Bethanne smacked Howard in the face with a sheet of wet newspaper.

"Cut it out!" he yelled, ducking to pick up something. Pokey snatched the newspaper from Bethanne and swatted Howard across the back. He turned on her and hit her in the neck with a soggy sweat sock.

Furious, she grabbed for the sock, which he was flicking like a towel. It snapped against her ear.

Bethanne picked up the newspaper again, and began to pound Howard on the back with it, over and over.

Meanwhile, Frankie had started to run for his bike,

with Tina and Joanne Schultz racing after him. Tony Murch had a face full of mud and brown grass that he was trying to wipe clean while fending off Steffie with the other hand.

Alan Foster shoved Bethanne away from Howard and yanked him by the arm.

"Let's go," he panted, sounding disgusted. "Boy, do they fight dirty."

"Oh, yeah?" Bethanne snarled. "Well, who started it?"

"Just for that," Howard gasped, "we're not going to help you anymore." He trudged off after Alan and Tony.

"Very funny," shouted Tina, as she passed them on her way back to the girls. "You're a big bunch of slobs, just trying to ruin everything."

"Aww, shut up," muttered Howard, waving his hand in disgust.

The girls crowded together and watched the boys climb onto their bikes and pedal slowly off down Mill Road. They hunched over their handlebars, keeping their heads down in the rain.

Pokey leaned against Nora's shoulder, trying to catch her breath.

"What started that?" she gasped.

"I don't know," panted Nora. "Didn't you see?"

Pokey shook her head. She looked at Nora and giggled. Nora was soaking wet, her blouse clinging to her skin, her slacks stained with grass, mud and something black and oily looking. Her red hair was a mass of damp coils plastered against her head and neck.

Nora stared at Pokey and began to giggle too.

"Do I look as bad as you do?" Pokey asked.

"You look *terrible*," Nora laughed.

"Well, we took care of *them*," sniffed Tina. She brushed her hands together briskly.

"That'll teach them," Joanne agreed, "to start up with *us*."

"You know," said Pokey, "I'm starved. We should have brought along a picnic lunch or something." She rubbed her stomach yearningly, thinking of how good a chicken salad sandwich would taste.

Her stomach rumbled.

"Anybody have any money?" Bethanne asked. "We could stop at the pizza place on the way home."

Steffie searched her pockets and pulled out a quarter. Nora found a quarter and a dime. No one else had anything.

"Well, we can all share, and chip in to pay Nora and Steffie back," Bethanne suggested.

The girls got their bikes and walked to the corner. When the light turned green, they walked across the street, then rode down the sidewalk, two by two, until they got to the Pizza Palace, on the corner of Mill Road and Pittsburgh Avenue.

They left their bikes outside and crowded into the tiny store.

Bethanne plunked the quarters and the dime on the counter. The man behind the counter stared at the bedraggled girls and scowled.

"One piece of pizza," Bethanne said. "And six napkins." She glanced at the price list on the wall. "And a small grape drink."

Joanne started to giggle. Pokey and Nora took a look at each other and Pokey covered her mouth with her hand.

The man slapped a piece of pizza down on the counter and shoved a small paper cup at Bethanne.

"Everyone take very small bites," she ordered. She nibbled off a corner and passed the pizza to Pokey. "That way we can each have two."

Pokey took a little taste of the pizza. It was delicious, but made her feel even hungrier. Reluctantly she passed it to Nora.

"Oh, that's wonderful," Nora sighed, and passed it on to Joanne.

Pokey followed the shrinking piece of pizza longingly with her eyes. It tasted so good, and she'd had such a tiny piece.

It finally came back to her, and she took another small bite. She had a sip of grape drink, and felt thirstier than ever.

"Listen," the man said sourly, "are you kids gonna

be here all day with that one piece of pizza? You're taking up the whole place, you know."

"Well, really," Bethanne said haughtily. "We're paying customers."

"You're paying for one customer," the man retorted.

When they got outside it was still raining. They rode back down Pittsburgh Avenue with their heads ducked low to keep the rain out of their eyes.

Instead of all going back to Bethanne's house, they began to split up, and waving good-bye, went their own ways home.

Pokey rode on the sidewalk most of the way, since it was too hard to see cars coming while she was hunched over the handlebars.

When she got home her parents were waiting anxiously for her.

"Charlotte, you're a mess," her mother cried. "What happened to you?"

Pokey looked down at her shirt and slacks. They were covered with mud, stained with grass, and sticking to her like Saran Wrap.

"Why didn't you come home? It's pouring," her mother went on.

"That must have been one dirty lot," her father commented.

"It is," Pokey said, nodding her head quickly. She

didn't think her parents would like to hear about the fight.

"Did you do a good job cleaning it up?"

Cleaning it up!

Pokey's mouth opened wide. In all the excitement, they had completely forgotten why they'd taken that long trip to the bus garage in the first place. Not only hadn't they finished cleaning up the lot, but they had left their trash bags there, littering up the place even more. They'd left their project in worse condition than it was before they'd started.

"Charlotte, get out of those clothes, please," her mother said. "You're soaking wet. And take a shower."

Pokey trudged up the stairs. Her sneakers squished as she walked. She felt badly about not cleaning up the lot, as they had set out to do.

Then she thought of the way the boys had tried to make trouble, and how she and the others made them run. Pokey brightened up. After all, they'd only left a few plastic bags there, and even if they *had* forgotten to clean the lot, the bike hike had been wonderful.

They really ought to do it again sometime, Pokey thought.

She whistled as she peeled off her clothes and stepped into the shower.

9

AFTER HER SHOWER and a change of clothes, Pokey was hungrier than ever. Her mother made her some chicken noodle soup and a sandwich, and Pokey gobbled them down.

While she was finishing off a bowl of applesauce, Gordon came in with two big bags and dumped them on the table.

"Hey, look out," Pokey said. "You nearly put that in my dish."

"Are you back?" Gordon asked sourly.

"No, I'm not," Pokey retorted. "This is a mirage you're seeing."

You'd think, she said to herself, he'd remember that *I'm* entitled to live here too.

A moment later the doorbell rang. Gordon ignored it and continued to unload packages of Banana Chips, Sesame Crunch and Soya Bits from his bags. Mrs.

Bloom went to the door and came back, followed by George.

"Pokey," he said, glancing sideways at Gordon, "can I speak to you? *Alone*," he added.

Pokey looked at Gordon. He was paying no attention to George or anyone else. He was just pulling things out of bags and muttering to himself. Today, in the familiar surroundings of their own kitchen, the idea of Gordon being a criminal didn't seem quite real. A pain in the neck, yes. Weird, yes. But a criminal?

She led George into the den and shut the door.

He pulled a small, spiral-bound notebook out of his pocket.

"I didn't see you around," George whispered, opening his notebook, "so when Gordon left the house I followed him myself."

"George, I don't think —"

"The suspect went to the shopping center," George read from his notes. "The suspect went right into the health food store without waiting outside. I hid near the shoe store. The suspect came out of the health food store after a while and he was carrying two big bags. The suspect went home."

George smacked his notebook shut and stuck it back into his pocket.

"George," Pokey said impatiently, "I know all that. He's in the kitchen right now, taking all that stuff he bought out of the bags. He had a perfectly good reason for going to the health food store. He was buying things for his party tonight."

"Oh?" George was momentarily dejected. "But why," he said, brightening up, "did he buy stuff for a party there? No one gets health food for a party. You get potato chips, things like that. The whole thing was probably just an excuse, so he could case the joint some more."

"Well . . ." Pokey began doubtfully. It was true that she'd never been to a party where health foods were the only refreshments. But still, Gordon-the-vegetarian might feel that since it was *his* party, everyone had to eat what he thought they should.

"*Anyway*," George went on, "I'm going to keep the suspect under surveillance. I still think he's up to something."

"Will you stop calling my brother 'the suspect'!" Pokey snapped.

"But that's what he is," George replied mildly.

"Oh, do what you want," Pokey said. "I don't care."

George gave her a hurt look and turned to leave. "Okay then," he said, "I'll do it all myself. Maybe someday you'll thank me."

He walked out of the den and Pokey heard the front door slam. That George! She shook her head. He almost had her believing in his crazy idea. But that's all it was — a crazy idea. Gordon was no criminal.

Was he?

Pokey sat at the kitchen table as the party preparations went on around her. She barely heard her family's conversation, so deeply was she concentrating on the limerick she had to finish for the Brauschmeyer's Wienerwurst contest. The grand prize was a South Seas Adventure in Tahiti.

> *Brauschmeyer's Wienerwurst treats,*
> *Are the finest available meats,*
> *The Brauschmeyer label*
> *Belongs on your table,*

Pokey had to make up a last line. It wasn't easy, trying to think up something that would fit and make sense.

"But doesn't belong on your feets," she wrote. Pokey giggled. She was feeling very silly.

"Right next to the carrots and beets." Well, that wasn't quite so ridiculous but it didn't say anything much. Pokey furrowed her forehead. Now, think hard, she told herself. She wrote down another line.

"Hey, listen," she said to her parents. "How does this one sound?"

Brauschmeyer's Wienerwurst treats,
Are the finest available meats,
   The Brauschmeyer label
   Belongs on your table,
Like pillowcases belong with sheets.

Gordon scowled at her. "It sounds asinine," he snapped.

"Well, the idea is good," her mother began.

"You don't like it, right?" Pokey said.

"It doesn't fit the rhythm," Mrs. Bloom explained. "Maybe if you made it shorter —"

"Like pillows belong with sheets?" Pokey asked.

"Well," her mother said doubtfully.

"Can't you see we're busy?" Gordon exploded suddenly. "What's so important about bothering everybody with that junk now? Why don't you just get out of the way?"

Pokey's head jerked back as if Gordon had struck her. She hadn't been doing anything! She was just sitting there, quietly working on her limerick. She felt her eyes fill with tears, and she didn't know if she was hurt or furious. She jumped out of her chair and grabbed her sheet of paper. Whether they were tears of anger or not, she didn't want Gordon to see them.

"Charlotte, you stay here," her mother said gently. "You're not bothering anyone."

"I know when I'm not wanted," Pokey said, swallowing hard.

Mr. Bloom glared at Gordon. "You certainly are wanted. I enjoy listening to your limerick."

"That's all right," Pokey said, walking out of the kitchen with her head held high. "I'd just as soon work in my own room — *in private.*"

She ran up the stairs and slammed her door.

I wish I didn't have a brother, she muttered under her breath. I hope he *does* end up in jail.

She clapped her hand over her mouth. That was a terrible thing to wish for Gordon! He might be a rat, but her parents probably still cared about him a little. They'd be very upset if their son turned out to be a criminal.

Well, then, Pokey thought, I wish he'd go to Alaska. *Forever.*

At eight o'clock Mrs. Bloom coaxed Pokey downstairs and gave her the job of answering the door and hanging up coats. Pokey sat on the second step and waited for the doorbell to ring. Gordon was down in the basement, doing something with his records.

The guests started to arrive at eight-fifteen and then they all seemed to come in bunches. Pokey was kept very busy for a while, greeting people and stowing away their coats in the hall closet.

In spite of the fact that she was perfectly capable of opening the door and hanging up coats, Gordon kept popping up the stairs every time the bell rang.

"I'm *doing* it, Gordon," Pokey kept repeating, but her brother would just nod, and come right back up again when the bell rang.

Just when Pokey thought the last guest had arrived, the doorbell rang once more. Gordon was at her side quick as a flash, and he pushed past her to fling the door open.

"Hi," he said, sounding almost breathless. "I thought you weren't coming."

A tall, blond girl stepped inside and smiled faintly at Gordon. Pokey frowned in bewilderment. There was something familiar about her; she wasn't one of Gordon's friends, but Pokey had the oddest feeling she'd seen her before.

"Oh, are you Gordon's parents?" the girl asked.

Pokey turned around to find her mother and father standing behind her in the hall.

"I'm Greta Hansen."

"Hello," Mrs. Bloom said pleasantly. "You must be a new friend of Gordon's. We haven't seen you around here before."

"Yes. We just moved here a couple of months ago. My father runs the new health food store in the shopping center. You know, Hermes' Health Food Heaven?"

The health food store! Of course, Pokey thought, that's where I saw her. She came out to talk to Gordon the other day, when he looked so suspicious.

Pokey's father and mother exchanged knowing looks.

"Oh, the health food store," Mr. Bloom said, as if he had suddenly solved a perplexing mystery. Pokey looked curiously at her parents. They smiled at each other. Why were they acting so oddly, Pokey wondered. And why had Gordon invited the daughter of the store owner to his party? Could it be, she thought darkly, that he wanted to worm his way into her confidence, to find out all the inside information about Hermes'?

Could it be that George was right after all? The whole thing began to seem real again.

But why were her parents smiling?

"Well, come on," Gordon said finally. "Everyone's downstairs."

Greta followed him to the basement.

"Well, that's that," said Pokey's father cheerfully. "I guess they don't need us around anymore."

"I'm sure they don't," agreed Mrs. Bloom.

"Anyone for a game of Crazy Eights?" asked Mr. Bloom.

"Me," Pokey said immediately. "At a dollar a point you owe me fourteen thousand and eighty dollars so far." Pokey had kept a running total for several years now, and even though she never expected him to actually pay up, she liked the idea of her father owing her all that money.

"That much?" he said unbelievingly. He always said that. He also always lost, which was why Pokey enjoyed playing with him. Her mother always won, or almost always.

Twice during the evening, Mrs. Bloom let Pokey go down to the basement with extra dishes of Soya Bits and raw vegetables. All the noise and music and laughter down there made Pokey feel a little bit left out.

Both times Pokey looked in on the party, Gordon was standing near the phonograph, hands in his pockets, looking glum. He certainly didn't seem to be having a good time. Everyone else was dancing or clustered together in little groups, talking and laughing. Greta kept dancing with one of Gordon's friends, Roger somebody, and Pokey saw that Gordon never stopped looking at them.

Perhaps his plan isn't working out the way he wanted it to, Pokey guessed. Maybe that's why he looks so unhappy. She certainly doesn't seem to be paying much attention to him. And if she doesn't pay any attention to him, how can he worm his way into her confidence?

It's just as well, Pokey decided, that he can't.

For his own sake.

When she was no longer interested in seeing what

was happening at the party, and when her father had lost sixteen dollars more to her at Crazy Eights, Pokey went up to her room to finish her limerick.

She finally came up with a last line, and read the whole limerick aloud to herself.

> Brauschmeyer's Wienerwurst treats,
> Are the finest available meats,
>   The Brauschmeyer label,
>   Belongs on your table,
> Like blankets belong on sheets.

Well, it's not terrific, Pokey admitted to herself, but it's the best I can do.

Along with her entry, she had to write the words "Brauschmeyer's Wienerwurst" on a plain piece of paper. Pokey tore up three pieces of paper before she was able to write "Brauschmeyer's Wienerwurst" without any spelling mistakes.

She looked at her entry again before she put it in the envelope. She really wasn't too confident that it was good enough to win a South Seas Adventure in Tahiti.

Well, I'll just have to concentrate all the harder, Pokey thought.

Concentrate!

With a gasp, Pokey realized she hadn't been using

her concentrated mind power since, since — she couldn't remember since when!

Oh, this is terrible, Pokey thought. Now I'll never win my dream house, or my dune buggy, or anything! Someone who had concentrated every day, for weeks and weeks without fail, will win all those prizes.

Virginia Hopewell had been right — it was much easier to forget about concentrating than to remember.

10

"I'LL TAKE SOME EGGS," Gordon said at breakfast the next morning.

Pokey looked up from her plate.

"Aren't you a vegetarian anymore?" she asked.

"No," he said sharply. "I'm not." He went through the pantry, collecting boxes of Banana Chips, tiger's milk mix, Soya Bits, and All-Gran Cereal. With a flourish, he dumped the armful of health foods into the metal garbage pail.

"There!" he said decisively. "That takes care of that."

Pokey's parents gave each other one of those looks that Pokey could never figure out.

"What about building stong muscles, teeth and bones, Nature's way?" Mr. Bloom asked.

"Leonard!" Pokey's mother glared at him.

"A lot of garbage," Gordon muttered.

After breakfast Gordon went outside with his basketball. They could hear the bounce, bounce, thunk of the ball as he shot baskets in the driveway.

"Well," said Pokey's mother, heaving a sigh of relief.

"I guess Gordon is finished going through his phase," Pokey remarked.

"He's finished going through *that* phase," her father agreed. "There may well be others."

"Well, at least," Pokey said, "he's not going to take up a life of crime."

"A life of crime!" her mother exclaimed. "Charlotte, wherever did you get an idea like that?"

"Well, from the way he was acting," Pokey said. "Hanging around that health food store all the time, and pretending to be interested in that stuff, and that girl — well, George thought he was planning a caper."

It sounded pretty silly, now that she was saying it out loud to her parents. And by the expressions on their faces, she knew they thought it was pretty silly too.

"Well, he was acting suspicious. And why else would he hang around that store all the time? I mean, if he wasn't casing the joint?" she finished lamely.

Her father was trying not to laugh, she could tell.

"Pokey, you really jump to conclusions," he said, shaking his head. "Your brother was simply going through the first pangs of unrequited love."

"Love? *Gordon?*" Pokey couldn't believe it. What

did love have to do with hanging around a store, and drinking healthshakes? And what in the world did "unrequited" mean?

"That's why he was always at the store," her mother explained. "Greta probably helps out there. And why he kept buying all the health food, and trying to live the way he thinks she does. He wanted to get to know her better, and to show her they had something in common."

Pokey frowned. "That's *dumb*," she declared.

Gordon, doing all that for love? Gordon, even *being* in love? After a moment's thought, Pokey decided that it was easier to believe that Gordon was a criminal.

She peered out the kitchen window at her brother, as if seeing a whole new person. He *looked* the same. He was dribbling the ball around in front of the garage, and jumping up for shots.

George was sitting on the steps in front of his kitchen door, watching Gordon's every move. He was making notes in his little notebook.

Pokey grinned. She could just imagine what George was writing.

"The suspect dribbled the basketball. The suspect shot baskets."

George was going to be pretty disappointed, she thought, that his suspect wasn't a suspect anymore.

The doorbell rang, and Pokey turned away from the window.

Her mother came into the kitchen a moment later, holding an envelope and looking puzzled.

"Charlotte, it's a special delivery letter for you. Registered."

"Registered? What's that?"

"It's a special way to send mail. I had to sign for it so they'll know you received it. What in the world could it be?"

"Well, hurry and open it!" her father said impatiently.

Pokey tore the envelope open and unfolded the letter inside.

"Dear Miss Bloom:" it said.

"We are delighted to inform you that you have won fourth prize in our Redimix Cake Mix Contest . . ."

The typewritten letters swan in front of Pokey's eyes. She had to read the first sentence over twice before she understood what it said.

"I won!" she screamed. "I won a contest!"

She grabbed her mother's arm and practically shoved the letter in her face.

"Read it!" she cried. "Read it! I can't — tell me what it says! What's my prize?" She began to whirl around the kitchen like a crazily spinning top, bumping into cabinets, the refrigerator — anything that got in her way.

"A transistor radio," her mother said.

"A TRANSISTOR RADIO!" Pokey screamed. "I won! I won just what I always wanted! And I didn't even *concentrate* on that."

"I don't believe this," her father said, looking over

the letter. "You actually won something in one of these contests? I never thought anybody —"

"What kind of a contest was it?" her mother asked, sinking down into a chair, as if her legs would no longer support her.

"I had to tell," Pokey panted, "why I liked Redimix Cake Mix in twenty-five words or less."

"Charlotte, that's amazing," her mother marveled. "You wrote something that good, that it actually won a prize. Think of all the adults who must have entered that contest."

"What did you write?" asked her father.

"Oh, I don't even remember," Pokey gasped. "Wait, let me think a minute." She fell into a chair and closed her eyes. "Oh, yeah. I like Redimix Cake Mix because it's so easy, even a child could make a beautiful birthday cake for her mother to remember long after the last delicious crumbs were eaten."

"Oh, Charlotte," her mother said softly.

Mr. Bloom threw open the window. "Gordon!" he shouted. "You'll never believe this! Your sister won a contest."

The ball fell out of Gordon's hands; he didn't even bother to pick it up.

George jumped up and came racing toward the window, his notebook and pencil forgotten.

"Are you kidding?" Gordon asked.

"Pokey, you won!" George yelled. "What did you win?"

"A transistor radio!" Pokey shouted back. "My very own transistor radio!"

"Wow!" George howled. "That's really something!"

Gordon came charging through the kitchen door, with George right behind him.

"You mean to tell me, you actually *won* one of those crazy contests? You actually *won something?*"

"See for yourself," Pokey said grandly, taking the letter from her father and handing it to Gordon.

"Dear Miss Bloom," Pokey quoted. "That's me."

"Good grief," Gordon muttered, rereading the letter twice. "She finally won something."

"Yeah," Pokey sighed. "Maybe I have good luck after all."

"It had nothing to do with luck," her father said sternly. "This wasn't a raffle. There was work and skill involved here. You had to think up something *good* to win that prize."

"Well —" Pokey felt herself bursting with excitement. She felt proud, and she knew her family was proud of her too. She looked at her mother and father, and George, all smiling as if they'd never frown again.

She looked at Gordon. His eyes were almost closed, his forehead furrowed in concentration.

"Gordon?" she said. "What's the matter?"

"How did that go?" he asked absently. "That liverwurst limerick?"

"Oh, you mean Brauschmeyer's Wienerwurst treats?"

"Yeah, yeah, that's it. How did it go?"

"Brauschmeyer's Wienerwurst treats, Are the finest available meats — I went over it so often," she interrupted herself, "I know it by heart."

"Go on, go on," Gordon said impatiently.

"The Brauschmeyer label belongs on your table . . ."

"Hmm," Gordon muttered thoughtfully. "Instead of the starches and sweets? No, that's no good."

"Good Lord," his father groaned. "It's an epidemic."

"Shh!" Gordon protested. "I'm thinking."

Pokey looked at her brother and grinned. Abruptly the picture of her dream house came into her mind.

I guess, she thought fondly, he doesn't have to live in the dungeon.